BLOOD DOCTRINE

Re-Education is in Order

MAQUEL A. JACOB

MAJart Works
Oregon, USA

MAJart Works
2001 NW Aloclek Dr #211
Hillsboro, OR 7124
www.majartworks.com

Publisher's Note: This is a work of fiction. Names, characters, places, and incidents are a product of the author's imagination. Locales and public names are sometimes used for atmospheric purposes. Any resemblance to actual people, living or dead, or to businesses, companies, events, institutions, or locales is completely coincidental.

Cover Art by Dar Albert

www.wickeddesigns.com

Book Layout ©2015 BookDesignTemplates.com

Ordering Information:
Quantity sales. Special discounts are available on quantity purchases by corporations, associations, and others. For details, contact the "Special Sales Department" at the address above.

Blood Doctrine/ Maquel A. Jacob -- 1st ed.
ISBN 978-0-9979564-1-0

WHAT LIES WITHIN

For all the tragic souls who volunteered to beta read my first vampire novel and gave me uncensored feedback. My gratitude is infinite. Sarah Walker, John H. Howard, Kat Baird, Nathan Miller. And, of course my mother, Camille Robinson.

I cherish you all.

For those who cherish the darkside and all its creatures who lurk within but also aknowledge that love knows no bounds. For even darkness cannot survive without a mate.

–MAQUEL A. JACOB

ONE: PLANNING

MAQUEL A. JACOB

"Yes, we all understand the problem," Count Ambrook snapped.

"We used to be feared by humans even with the treaty in place." Queen Celeste frowned.

"A certain aesthetic was expected when we roamed into the streets," Count Sapienti added.

"This new generation of vampires has tainted our status almost beyond repair."

Count Sapienti cleared his throat, getting their attention. He was older in terms of when he had been turned. It gave him an air of sophistication the others tried to match. Count Ambrook quelled his envy. This man was part of the goal. When Count Sapienti began to speak, they all seemed to lean towards his voice.

"I have gone over all the proposals and have come up with a remedy. First order of business is to get them out of the eyes of society. They need to be isolated in order for this to work."

"Those pampered whelps? They would never stand for it!"

"And whose fault is that?" Count Sapienti glared down the line of pale faces. When no one answered, he continued. "Education is key. The young ones have little or no knowledge of their clans' lineage. Presentation when outside the castle and feeding protocols also need to be addressed. To ensure compliance they would need guardians."

"Guardians from where? Surely you don't mean for some of the council to accompany them?"

"Of course not!" Count Sapienti squeezed the bridge of his nose with two fingers. "These guardians need to be capable of serving their wards in addition to protection."

"Protected from what, exactly?"

"My proposed location for this endeavor would be a neutral zone in the territory."

Sharp intakes of air filled the room. Count Ambrook knew that would be the reaction. Neutral zone or not, some humans still liked to hunt vampires for sport. He himself had scouted the building necessary for the project and found security measures wouldn't do much good. Sending their little blood-thirsty darlings off to fend for themselves was still a wonderful thought.

"An old boarding school has been acquired and is in the process of being renovated for our purposes. The government is leery of our agenda of course."

"Yes, yes! Back to this guardian thing. How are we to go about this?"

"Count Ambrook." Count Sapienti nodded, giving him the floor.

"We comb our armies for them."

"The lower class?" Queen Celeste exclaimed in disgust.

"Slaves, really," Count Durante snorted.

Count Ambrook closed his eyes in exasperation. They had all complained about the situation and he was elected under duress to find a solution, which he had with Count Sapienti. Now they balked at the plan.

"Do you wish to let it continue until it is too late to defend what is coming?" Silence again. "Yes, our slaves who we use to defend our covens. Do you have a different class in mind for this task? I didn't think so."

"The selection process?" Queen Erena asked.

"I will lay out the details within the week."

Yellow beams of light shot holes in the grey sky. They all jumped out of their seats, abandoning tea and hors de oeuvres. The legs of their chairs scraped against the hardwood floors as they were pushed back.

"As I said before, it's getting late. We can continue this meeting another day."

Count Ambrook watched the row of gleaming expensive vehicles pull away in haste from his castle's courtyard. Off in the distance to his right he caught his son running wildly to the side entrance, his horde of friends in tow. Many of his coven's high court were blond, beautiful and deadly which made him all the more disappointed with the young one's behavior. Laughter echoed up to him and he knew they had done something unthinkable, yet again. Their clothes were disheveled and his superior eyesight noticed the tiny splatters of blood adding to their wardrobe.

That will end soon enough.

Night brought a flurry of activity in the castle. Despite its massive size, the place felt crowded as everyone awoke refreshed and ready to start their evening. Count Ambrook sat up in his King-sized bed and leaned over until his head hit his knees. His mate lovingly rubbed his back. She knew his strife and supported his decision.

"Come, my love. You must get ready as well. We have to give the nightly address to the coven."

Her voice was husky and low. His groin tightened for a moment then relaxed. There was no time for that. Begrudgingly, he threw the covers off and slid out of bed naked. On cue, his butler entered with his wardrobe draped across one arm and shoes carried in the hand of the other.

Burgundy. Velvet no less.

"I know I requested something old school, but really, Hayes."

"Is it too much, master?"

Count Ambrook let out a small breath and shook his head.

"No, it's fine." He heard his wife snicker and turned to see her smooth hand clamped over her mouth to muffle laughter. "I will not be up there alone in mockery." Addressing his butler while pulling on his clothes, he said, "Make sure her handmaid understands our need to 'match'."

"Of course, master."

His butler bowed as he left and his wife gave him a dirty look. Shoes on, he headed out the bedroom.

"My love!" Her outcry made his hand stop on the door handle. "Are you going to go out with your hair in such disarray?"

Running both hands through his waist length hair, he straightened it out as much as possible.

"Does it really matter when I'm wearing this?"

"Hmm. No, I guess not." She made a small giggle, her eyes twinkling. "See you soon."

In the hall, he ran into his son's hall guard. The man looked haggard and irate.

"Is my son awake?"

"No, my lord. He and his friends claim exhaustion and request another hour of sleep."

"Get him up! And make sure they understand I will not tolerate such laziness in my coven!"

"Of course, my lord."

The guard bowed then turned back down the hall. Many of the Elders from the old days were getting frustrated with the new vampires. His son was all of fifty-two years old and a pariah. That was within the age range of the problem; 45-60. In a short period of time his compatriots' offspring along with his own had dismantled the legacy of vampires throughout the countryside.

Random attacks, lack of social grace, clothes that would make any aristocrat shudder in horror. There was one incident where his son had gone out hunting and not bathed for days after. The stench lingered to the point of getting his attention. Enraged, he made him and his friends line up along the castle walls outside to let the servants power hose them down. The memory angered him all over again.

Within the hour, his coven had assembled in the great hall. Seated on the platform high above, he was able to get a good look at them. Beside him, his wife grimaced in her velvet Burgundy dress, visibly uncomfortable. Her chocolate colored hair hung loose draped around her shoulders. His inner council gave nods of approval for their attire. In the back of the hall, he spotted his son who was supposed to be in front along with the other high class children sneaking in. Letting it go, he started.

"Greetings my beloved coven. I hope this night fares you well."

He went into his normal speech of acceptable behavior, observing the few who rolled their eyes in defiance and made note. He couldn't even hear his own voice, a vacuum of silence enveloped him. Snorting from the back broke it. There was no need to see from where it came. Pursing his lips, he halted his instructions. The coven went silent and they all stared up at him, curious. The ones snickering in the back also stopped and his glare bore into them like hot coals. His son frowned before turning his head away. Count Ambrook resumed, and when he was finished, stood to signal dismissal. As his horde left to their own devices, he reached for his wife's hand and squeezed. She returned it in fervor. This was not going to be an easy transition.

Black sleek metal glinted in the moonlight as it came careening up the driveway to the courtyard. Count Sapienti's giant Bentley had arrived. At the front doors, two footmen exited the vehicle to let out its occupants. He rose out followed by his wife, an accountant and his butler. Count Ambrook waited patiently for them to get closer before offering a greeting. The man looked equally worn for wear. Staying up past dawn on gloomy days caused havoc on their biological clocks.

"Count Sapienti, how does the night find you?"

"Weary," was his reply.

"I concur."

The two coven leaders clasped hands while their wives embraced each other. Entering the castle, the butlers tended to their masters respectively and the hall guards led the entourage to the sitting room on the second level of the far wing. A tray with snifter glasses and a bottle of fine bourbon sat on the coffee table between the two large upholstered chairs in the center. Two smaller seats were arranged on each side. Both Counts occupied the main chairs.

"So," Count Sapienti began while the bourbon was being poured, "How is the school coming?"

"Renovations are on schedule. We still need to find instructors and someone to handle curriculum."

"Hmm. Yes."

The bourbon was distributed and they all took a sip. No one spoke for a long time.

"I think it may be best if we have a mix of old guard and some of the not so new generation to teach," Count Ambrook's wife finally said.

"Not a bad idea. The hundred and up club can shed some light on how times have changed in regards to us old ones." Count Sapienti took another sip.

"Speak for yourself!" His wife straightened her bodice.

"I am not yet half a millennium."

Count Sapienti made a sideward glance at her then gave his attention to his accountant.

"How are we on budget?"

"With contributions from all eight covens, we should be good for at least twenty years."

"Is that enough time to reeducate those ungracious hoodlums?"

"I like to think of them as unrefined. They are still new to this." Count Sapienti's wife looked away after saying that as she sipped her bourbon.

"Pigs in mud have more dignity than our offspring at this point," Count Sapienti scoffed.

"Don't let Queen Erena hear you say that about her precious daughter," his wife said.

"Trust me," Count Ambrook said, "she knows all too well."

"But really, the neutral zone?" Countess Sapienti asked. "It's actually more cost effective than you think." The accountant shifted in his seat so that he could see them all at once. "And, the government will recognize it as a private boarding school."

"Ahh, a tax incentive." Count Ambrook nodded. "Remember when taxes on property were around ten dollars?" Count Sapienti laughed.

"Now, you're just showing your age."

Count Sapienti took on a more serious tone.

"When can we start filling it up?"

"After we get guardians for them and they are well acquainted. I say in about ten years."

"We must coordinate in addressing our covens."
"Agreed. Rebellion?"

Count Sapienti smiled. "I do not let my young ones dictate or overrun my authority."

They all took another sip, eyeing each other with equal conviction. Count Ambrook feared he may have to harm his own coven to get their plan in motion. A necessary sacrifice, even if it had to be his son.

CHOOSING CANDIDATES

Dirt floors, cobwebs and a stagnant smell assaulted Count Ambrook as he reached the lower level of the castle where his army and lower class servants resided. He hadn't been down there in over fifty years and ashamed to see its state. As a proud coven, this would not do. The rooms were caves with makeshift furniture littering each one. He passed a large cave housing mounds of armor. Four servants were going to task cleaning them one by one. They wore long dirty hemp woven tunics and their hair was tangled from lack of maintenance. Producing a handkerchief, he covered his nose to block the aroma of decay.

At last, he came to an alcove that led to the arena. Walking into the dusty place, he looked around. The seating above was on the verge of crumbling and the arena floor itself was not level. It didn't surprise him since the last time they held an official battle for rank was well over a century ago. Yet, he could tell it had seen some action over the last few decades and that sent alarms off in his head. Unsanctioned fighting amongst his coven was forbidden. A glance at his tour guide affirmed his suspicions, the guard quickly looking away out of guilt.

"How many are eligible for fighting status?" "Maybe about a hundred or so," the guard answered. "Army candidates?"

"Lower class servants? I believe about forty."

"I want them. That way we don't deplete our army numbers. See to it."

"You want me to get them now?"

Count Ambrook's eyes turned red with anger and he hissed.

"Yes, soldier. Now."

With not much blood in the man to begin with, he couldn't get any paler, but his fear was visible.

"Yes, my lord. Right away." The guard spun on his heels and left the room.

Old blood permanently stained the cavern's golden amber rock surface. Count Ambrook placed a hand over his face. It was about to get even more stained. First, repairs were in order then he would get it sandblasted afterwards.

Huddles of filthy vampires stood scattered about the cavernous arena during the early hours of night. Count Ambrook surveyed each one, trying to pick any that he deemed worthy of even participating in the events. Of the forty, sadly, none caught his interest. His enforcer tsked at the lot.

"What a piss poor group of garbage. I can't imagine any one of them capable of guarding our young heirs."

"I agree, yet we must. More training may be necessary." He took a closer inspection as he walked among them. "Why do they seem malnourished? Who oversees feeding them?"

A guard in dingy battle armor stepped up from the ranks.

"That would be me, my lord."

"Explain this!"

"Some of them are greedy, so we have to ration out the provisions."

"And you force them to battle in this condition as well?"

"We," the guard stopped.

"I want them cleaned up and ready for combat within the year. This arena must be brought up to standards." He focused his attention on the decrepit group of lower class slaves. "A new order will be implemented in the coming years and my son requires a guardian. You will all compete for that position and the winner will gain status in my inner sanctum." Nothing registered in their eyes. "Those who come close will get better quarters and a rise in status." Still no reaction.

Count Ambrook turned and walked back to his enforcer. Getting within earshot, he leaned close to him.

"What the hell is going on?" His enforcer's eyes narrowed.

"I think they are so far gone that they are numb. Hunger, fear and poverty can do that to a being."

"I should have been watching my coven more closely."

"You cannot be in every crevice of the castle. This is not of your doing."

"Then whose is it? Their lives are my responsibility."

A feeling of distress came over him. There was no excuse for such neglect. As one of the three ruling covens he had a duty to show strength and compassion. His coven was his extended family and he was clear on how the classes should work. When slaves were not happy, they eventually rebeled and he did not want that on his conscience. Count Sapienti's words echoed in his head.

Count Sapienti's castle was a construct of black marble spiraling towards the sky, fortuitously blocking the sun. Green pasture surrounded its base creating a stark visual contrast. Inside its walls lay a maze of rooms arranged in no particular kind of uniformity. Whenever someone rose in class they would find a place within the castle and carve out their new abode. Despite the chaotic layout, there was a flow.

Falson Spienti, heir to the coven, paced his overly large bed chamber. Wearing leggings and a dark robe, he had no desire to dress like the hip human rich kids, finding their attire constricting. His dark hair always hung loose in deep waves below his shoulders because women loved to run their fingers through it. Booze, hunting and making an ass of yourself in public was not his idea of fun. Hunting for a ripe piece of ass was another story. That was his vice.

The sound of footsteps echoed and judging by the resonance, still a ways down the hall. He smiled. A secret meeting with yet another princess was about to be underway. She was from one of the lower houses and probably a half breed but that wasn't a deterrent. His father constantly chastised him on this, citing a strain on coven relations. What different did it make if the princesses wanted to spread their pale thighs for him? And that whole respect for the old ways was literally getting old.

His chamber door flew open revealing a dark blond female in a long dress with corset. Her bosom was pushed so far up they almost touched her chin. She seemed out of breath, the mounds heaving in fast succession, but the smile on her face was devious.

This one should be fun.

He pulled her into the bedroom and slammed the door shut.

Eyes blood red, Count Sapienti thundered down the corridor. When the messenger came from the seventh coven informing him that their princess had gone missing and asked all covens for assistance, he knew immediately where she was. This had happened on too many occasions and he was now fed up. The schooling plan could not come fast enough. Two of his enforcers followed closely behind ready to do his bidding.

Reaching his son's door, he kicked it open with one foot, busting it off its hinges. It skid across the floor into the far wall. There on the bed he found his son enjoying a ride from the missing princess. Before the startled naked couple could react, he grabbed the girl by the hair and flung her off the bed. She hit the floor with a smack, his son's still erect man- hood instantly exposed. He wrapped his hands around his son's neck lifting him vertically off the bed and did the same.

The princess spun up onto her hands and knees hissing, her fangs protruding. He leaned forward and backhanded her into a wall that buckled from the impact.

"You dare to sneak into my house and taint it with your selfish morals. I will not have a war between covens because you can't keep your legs close, opening them up for anyone who's stupid enough to want your dried up cunt!"

His son recovered and crawled back to the edge of his bed.

"Father," he started.

"You! Do not speak!" Count Sapienti gestured to his enforcers. "Get her out of my castle."

They took one arm each and hauled her off with her clothes in a heap covering her breasts.

"Father," his son tried again.

Count Sapienti exited the room without saying another word. He was more furious than normal and attributed it to the plan being implemented. By the time he rounded the corner, two different enforcers came into step behind him. Instead of going up, he detoured to the stairwell that led down to the lower class dwellings.

Battle cries assaulted his ears as he got closer to the underground caged arena. Most covens forbade infighting but he felt it kept his people on their toes.

They went up or down in class rank depending on their performance. Lights came into view at the end of the stairwell and he saw the place was packed. Two male vampires were in the arena covered in each other's blood, ready to pounce. He walked right up to the edge of the cage as the one closest to him launched into the air and struck down the other.

The arena fell into a hush and the fighter with his fist still raised halted as he caught his master out of the corner of his eye. The Count waved him away and stepped into the cage. He did a slow 360 degree turn in the center, getting a good look at the dingy, blood thirsty vampires in attendance.

"I have a proposal for those of you in the lowest ranks. In one year's time a position will open within my circle. Only the top ten from the battles hence forth will be eligible to compete for it." He watched their eyes go wide. "Yes. The winner will be a part of my upper echelon."

Loud roars of excitement shook the arena and Count Sapienti grinned. This made him feel much better. Even the downed vampire in the cage shook off his injuries and stood to chant with the rest of the horde.

"This must be kept in confidence here. None of the higher courts are allowed to participate. This offer stands only for you."

More cries, this time of appreciation. He could imagine the deviant plots going on in their heads as he left the cage and headed back to the stairwell.

"You have incited mayhem, my lord," the enforcer on his left said.

"All the better."

"May I ask why not even we are allowed?" the other en- forcer inquired.

"Because you have already shown your worth. I want someone who will fight fang and talon to get to this status."

De Luce Coven

One finger twisted around a blonde curl Princess Adelia chewed her bottom lip as she tilted her head to one side. With her other hand, she tapped the jewel encrusted dagger against her thigh.

"I think," she said, "I'll see what happens there."

She thrust the dagger into the pale thigh in front of her and listened intently to the muffled screams of her prey. The young male dangled from her bedroom ceiling, his own underwear wadded up in his mouth. Multiple wounds were seeping blood down his body and onto the floor. Adelia leaned forward and licked the deep cut she'd made, slurping a good amount of blood into her mouth.

"Princess! You mustn't!"

Her handmaid stood in the doorway with that ghastly look she always had on her face when the Princess brought home a play toy. She strode across the room and went to cut the ties holding her victim suspended. Adelia's face turned ugly, wrinkled and her red eyes burned. Her talons grew as she grabbed the handmaid by the head. She began screaming, tendrils of red lining her face as they pierced skin.

"How dare you," Adelia seethed. "I am daughter to the Queen, you heifer! I do as I please." She let the woman go by tossing her away. "You don't order me."

The ties snapped and the young man went tumbling down. Adelia whirled around to see who had cut them and came face to face with one of her mother's enforcers. The woman was easily over six feet tall and wore body armor like a Valkyrie. Her blond hair was swooped back in the helmet and her grey eyes bore down on the princess. There was no need for them to glow red signaling rage. Before Adelia could speak, the enforcer scooped up the bloodied young man and exited the room.

"Give me back my toy!"

Adelia's voice boomed with guttural rage and she instantly regretted it as the enforcer halted. Fear gripped her. In most cases, she could do whatever she wanted, bribing or threatening the coven servants not to inform her mother. This was the first time one of mother's enforcers had come to her chamber unannounced. Something or someone must have tipped her off. She slid a side glance at the handmaid.

"Do not blame that servant girl for your mistake." Adelia's eyes widened with even more fear.

"You seem to not take into regard who you target for your fun. The Queen requests your presence immediately." The enforcer then turned her head back to look at her. "I would clean up first."

As the enforcer disappeared down the hall, Adelia screamed. The veins in her neck and hands bulged from rapid blood flow. She ran to her closet while stripping off her blood-stained dress then stood staring into its contents.

"Dignified! Docile!"

She angrily pushed and yanked pieces around until she found something she liked. Dressed in a modest black dress, she found a satin ribbon and used it to sweep her bright blond hair to one side tying a bow.

"Deep breaths."

Adelia did that four times before heading out.

The throne room was fairly dark. Red candles lit the way down the velvet carpet to the foot of the throne's platform. Sitting regal was her mother, Queen Erena, staring down at her with such disgust Adelia flinched. All of her mother's advisors and four enforcers were present awaiting her.

"Do you know why our castle is not attacked?" Adelia stopped her advance hearing her mother's tone. "There is a treaty. An agreement that we will not go off snatching the children of government leaders. Or any other children, for that matter." Her mother's gaze never wavered. "So imagine my surprise when I received a messenger at my castle doors informing me that someone from my coven was seen with the son of a senator. A young man who had gone missing yesterday."

Adelia felt her blood chill. It's true, she didn't really care who she brought here to play with because humans were only inferior beings and food. Politics never crossed her mind. The angry looks on her mother's inner circle let her know that she had done it this time.

"So, we have to make sure he is completely healed and force him to lie. Say he was invited for dinner and was having SO MUCH FUN that he forgot to let his family know where he was."

Her mother stood.

Everyone parted like the red sea as she neared the bottom and came to tower over her.

"Because the alternative would be a dissolution of the treaty and war between humans and vampires would come once again."

"They're just humans," Adelia stammered. "What do we care if they come after us?"

She felt her body hit the stone wall and tasted blood as it spewed out of her mouth. Bones had broken, she was sure of it. Her mother stood in the same spot as before, the back of her right hand slightly pink from making contact with her face.

"Confine her. I don't want to see her until the next new moon."

Queen Erena went back to her throne and her advisors began to bombard her with suggestions. Two of her enforcers dragged Adelia from the indentation on the wall and carried her away. Tears stung her eyes.

The Queen's head Advisor straightened his vest and cleared his throat.

"I believe we should get the ball rolling on selection sooner than later."

"I agree. It was suggested we comb our lower class." Her second advisor added.

"They would be more enthusiastic."

"How shall we go about this?" Queen Erena tried to brush off her anger.

"Instead of casting a wide net, I think we should look into the army officers' offspring."

"That is," Queen Erena looked up in contemplation. "More ideal."

"Did you want to inspect them?" The first advisor asked. "Go into the soldiers' quarters?" Queen Erena asked incredulously.

"Of course not, my Queen." He was appalled by his own suggestion.

"If you trust us to handle this, we shall not disappoint," her second advisor said.

"I do. See it done."

The soldiers' quarters were dank, smelling of wet stone and fur. Accompanied by one of the Queen's female enforcers, the head advisor stepped carefully along the tight corridor until they came to stop at a stone entrance. Pulling the lever on the side, the stone rolled away to expose a large mess hall filled with soldiers preparing for night duty. Some halted at his presence while others continued donning their equipment.

"Good evening, soldiers. I have come with a proposition from our Queen."

That got their attention. The head commander came out from behind his crew and stepped closer to him.

"What does our Queen need?"

"A new plan for the Princess and her court is being implemented soon. She will need a guardian for when she, on occasion, would be relocated to the neutral zone." Sharp hisses came in succession. "The Queen wants a battle to select the strongest of your offspring to fill the position."

"What need for a battle? My son is the strongest."

Yelling ensued about whose child was better suited and the enforcer squelched it by drawing her sword. The din lowered to silence.

"This is why a battle is needed. They must prove their worth. Of course, you will tell no one else. Only your group is privy to this."

"That is a wise decision."

"You have one year to complete the selection"

The head commander smirked. "Understood."

Ambrook Coven

Pristine stone freshly sandblasted greeted Count Ambrook as he made the final inspection of the fighting arena. A nod of approval came from his enforcers who accompanied him. Tonight, would be round one of the selection process and he made sure to be in attendance. The forty candidates showed signs of improvement health wise so there should be no issue with them going full strength.

"It's been a long time since we've hosted a battle. Too bad it is an internal one. I would have liked to see how they fared with the other covens." His head enforcer stepped up beside him.

"From what I have seen, not too well." Count Ambrook circled the arena while staring up into the seating section. "Will your daughter be participating in the schooling? I know she is not like the others but more knowledge never hurts."

"She is actually quite interested. Will she also need a guardian?"

"Of course. You get to choose from the top nine after the winner."

His enforcer stopped a few feet behind him. He turned and saw the revelation on the man's face.

"So there will be five from each coven attending this school. Why pick from the top ten? Take the five most ferocious and be done with it."

"We can do that as well but, it would make for better sport. And besides, you want to find the best fit for your child. Personality wise."

A hall guard came in and approached them. On bended knee, he spoke.

"The fighters are ready, my lord."

"Good. Shall we assemble our audience?" Count Ambrook addressed his enforcer.

At the stroke of midnight, the arena was filled to capacity with the coven's upper class along with high ranking soldiers. Four enforcers were in the pit acting as judges and referees. The first round would be a battle royale. Only the half left standing would advance to the second round while the rest went through another group battle until only ten remained. Then the top ten from both rounds would go against each other. By Count Ambrook's calculations, one battle a week should put them close to the deadline.

When the candidates came trudging in, he could feel the air deflate in the room. A sense of disappointment in the them permeated. Count Ambrook grimaced, hoping to see some good fighting and get the audience back in the spirit. The group was split up into groups of ten at each corner and awaited instruction.

"My family, I am pleased to give you some entertainment and a show of our strength this night. To my fighters," Count Ambrook made sure to eye all of them. "Show no mercy!"

He gestured to his lead enforcer. With the crack of his whip, he brought the group to attention.

"You will fight until you can no longer. No killing! We are family and do not murder our own. This round you go against all. Begin!"

He cracked his whip once more and to everyone's surprise, all forty exposed talons and fangs. Bodies leaped into the air and a clash of flesh resounded. Beautiful arcs of red flew around landing on the stone floor to create a splatter painting fit for an art gallery. The audience cheered and gyrated with excitement.

Much better.

Count Ambrook sighed with relief then joined in the shouting.

Sapienti Coven

Dungeons were good for some things and now served the purpose of housing the fighters wounded from the selection battle. Count Sapienti's head enforcer counted at least thirty vampires in the throes of recuperation. The wounds were deep, animalistic. He had known this would be the outcome when his master announced it. Dull minded embeciles with only blood and mayhem running through their veins did not seem ideal, but then again seeing the looks in their eyes, he thought differently.

With only the first few rounds complete, the numbers had dwindled significantly. Out of hundreds, there were now maybe sixty going the distance. Those who truly wanted it showed up for each battle. He wondered who would rise to the top ten.

Down the stairwell he went to witness the outcome of the fight going on at the moment. Loud cheers couldn't cover the sound of wet flesh tearing. He watched the two fighters collide with bone crushing force. One was a big towering wall of muscle, his neck nearly disappearing. The other was of normal size. Lean, well-built and lithe. He had dodged the giant's previous advance by flying effortlessly over him. A head on collision proved a bad idea on the giant's part because his opponent went for an underhanded blow. The sound of a snap was heard and the giant came away with a broken arm.

Angry, the giant roared. His thick fangs dripping with his opponent's blood, he charged. The younger fighter stood still until the last minute, letting the giant get almost too close. Crouching down ever so slightly, he leaped up and delivered a round house kick at the exact level of the giant's head and sent him flying into the metal bars of the cage. The giant lay still when he hit the floor.

A hush fell over the arena. Count Sapienti's head enforcer deduced that the young one was not favored to win. Finally, some cheers erupted and the fighter staggered backwards. Bloodied but still standing the edge of his mouth twitched upwards a little.

"Impressive," the head enforcer said to himself.

"Indeed."

He turned to see his counterpart standing next to him.

The other enforcer was stroking his chin in deep thought.

"He may be one to watch after all." "You know of this one?"

"He lost every battle up until now. The thing is, he kept competing."

"He wants this."

"More than we think."

The underdog fighter sat in his filthy stone quarters eating the rations left over from earlier. He didn't have much of an appetite after the last fight. He hated hurting his own kind for sport, moving up the ranks that way made him ill. But it was the way of life in the lower levels of the castle and this new proposal had him rethinking his position. To get that high up and serve the Count directly was an honor no one could pass up.

A hall guard came to his entrance and tapped the side of the stone with the butt of his gun. He hated those things too. Only the army carried both gun and sword. There was no honor in fighting anymore. Gunpowder had changed that centuries ago. Shoving the rest of his meal in his mouth, he brushed off his pants and followed him. If, in order to get out of the slums, he had to resolve to hurting his friends, so be it. Entering the cage, he saw the other four contenders waiting for him. Confused he looked to them for an answer. One of them shrugged, raising his arms halfway. The enforcer in charge of the fight came to the center of the ring.

"This will be the final battle. A battle Royale!"

Cheers erupted from the stands and he felt his blood chill. The initial fight was like that and he barely made it. His opponents didn't like it either, pursed lips all around.

"The previous victor gets to stand his ground in the center. Line it up!"

The other four spread out and stood at each corner surrounding him. A four on one assault.

Great.

"Begin!"

No time to come up with a plan, he watched the four leap at him with hungry eyes, fangs and talons already extended. The first few bouts were going to hurt.

"The Victor!"

The enforcer had his hand closed around his wrist, which was the only thing holding him up. His body was battered, bloody and screaming in pain but he endured. There was no way he would give the audience who despised him the satisfaction of seeing his agony. No one cheered for him. Instead, there were boos, curses and trash thrown down, raining into the cage.

He was no one. A dirty slave living in the slums who fought for food and minimal status. Many of the vampires he had beaten were part of some clique in the upper echelon or seasoned fighters constantly fluctuating on the status ladder.

Suddenly, silence.

One of the downed fighters raised himself up, ready to pounce when a shiny boot slammed on his head, sending him back onto the cage floor. Count Sapienti had arrived.

"You disrespect the victor? Did any of you defeat him? He is the only one deserving his prize. I watched him rise above all others while many of you gave up."

The Count held out a hand to him and he took it. "Come. Let us get you cleaned up. You have much to do in the coming years."

"Yes, your grace." He barely got the words out, his throat raw from yelling.

As they walked out of the arena and into the stairwell that led up, Count Sapienti whispered to him.

"You did well to stay standing in the state you're in."

A medical team met them halfway and he gladly fell into their waiting arms.

"Make sure he is treated and fed." They nodded in response.

That was the last thing he heard or saw. Pain took him into darkness.

De Luce Coven

Queen Erena held court for the end of night and listened intently to her council report on the events that transpired. Luckily, her daughter had not gone trolling through the streets in search of playthings or caused any incidents. She was a princess and had to be given some respect but not at the level she dictated. Queen Erena knew it was her fault for creating the spoiled and vicious child but now there was a chance to remedy that.

"Would you like a report on the selections, my Queen?"

"Is it going well?"

"It seems so."

"Then no. Unless something unprecedented occurs, I just need to know who the winner is when the time comes."

"What if the princess does not approve?"

The Queen lifted her head off her upraised hand and glared at her advisor. Her court reared back from the throne.

"I have no desire to accommodate her wishes on this matter. She will do as she is told."

"Of course, my Queen. My apologies."

"Where is that little deviant?"

The advisor looked towards the others and then back at the Queen.

"Flirting?"

Her eyes glowed red. Yes, when her child was not being sadistic she was trying to get some willing participant to fall between her legs. The girl assumed she had no knowledge of this but since the start of the plan, the Queen had her enforcers keeping watch. Locking her away would be counterproductive so she had to endure it for now. The only consolation was that most men steered clear of her daughter, not the least bit attracted to her personality which turned them off physically.

"What are we even fighting for?" The son of a soldier asked.

"It is for your Queen! No matter what the cause." His father whacked him in the back of the head. "It was her personal request."

"Then we fight. I won't hold back because we are cousin." The man next to him remarked.

"I wouldn't have it any other way."

Another fighter looked up from reading a book and snorted as they passed him into the battle chamber. Whatever the reason, he would wipe out both their asses in the field. Getting on the Queen's good graces was not to be taken lightly. He shut the book and headed down to join the rest of the fighters. Whoever won this round was going to go up against him next.

Unlike the others, he didn't go by speculation. Instead, he had crept around his father undetected and listened to the conversation he had between the other high ranked officers whose children were slotted to fight. Neutral zones and the Princess' guardian were the main topic. He still didn't have a clear picture but that was enough. An explanation was sure to come after he claimed victory.

Which he found fairly easy to do once he got into the top five. The final battle pitted him against the General's son who in his cockiness shot his mouth off incessantly between bouts. His friends and the other high rank officers cheered him on, entertained by his jesting. As the son of a lieutenant, the fighter had no one in his corner. His father watched silently, a smoldering threat daring him to lose, the consequences of failure dire. He was not supposed to have made it this far, the other high rank children obvious shoe ins.

Tired of playing the general's son's game, he went full battle mode. Sword, fangs and talons went at the unsuspecting son. He caught his countering rhythm too late and the fighter ended the battle with the general's son lying bloody and broken on the field.

Only a few scratches here and there marred his own skin.

All the cheering had ceased and the onlookers stood stunned. The general went to get his son but the enforcers refereeing the event stopped him, letting the medical group handle the wounded.

"Congratulations, you have proven yourself worthy of the Queen's court."

He bowed using his entire upper body. When he raised his head, he saw his father leave the battlefield. A tiny smirk tugged at the corners of his mouth and the fighter smiled. His father would get promoted and his mother will have new quarters in the upper levels of the castle.

"You must rest and heal. In a few days' time, you will be presented to the Queen for instructions."

"Thank you." He bowed again and followed the servant waiting to lead him back in.

Ambrook Coven

Every time the rations were distributed it became commonplace to add more during the fights. Hunting was up by twenty percent but it was all for a great cause. The guards in charge of feeding the fighters went hunched over in the low ceiling cave down the row handing out portions. As they got closer to the end, the second guard stopped his partner.

"Don't feed that one. He's a greedy one. Chancellor says to only give him two a day."

"The others get five to keep up their strength," the sec- ond said in defiance.

"You want to disobey the Chancellor, go ahead."

The second guard looked at the fighter in question. Relatively small, he may even be called somewhat pretty, his face was dirty and eyes listless.

"Hungry," the little one whispered.

"Sorry, kid. Got orders."

A tear ran down his face. Wearing raggedy shirt and pants, the fighter resembled an abandoned child from the city slums. The second guard felt sorry for him until he realized this kid had won more than a few fights on half rations. It was inconceivable.

"Hang in there."

The Chancellor watched from the entryway of the fighters staging cave and tapped his bottom lip thinking about that young fighter. Something was very off about him. He also thought his winning streak strange. His assistant came up behind him.

"You asked for me, my lord?"

"I want you to test the DNA of that fighter." He pointed to the little one.

"Looking to adopt a new child?"

"That is no child. He eats more than any of us and yet when you starve him, he is no less strong."

His assistant frowned.

"Very unusual. He's so small."

"Just get it done. Quickly."

The horn sounded, signaling the start of a new battle and the Chancellor went around to his seat in the cheering section. Count Ambrook was already there with his wife and he bowed to him.

"Another round of debauchery for you and the lady, my lord?"

Count Ambrook smirked.

"It is fascinating to see the ones with determination lose."

"Yes, well let's see who comes out the victor tonight." Three fights in and the little one came into the ring. The Chancellor scooted forward and leaned over the ledge. He could feel Count Ambrook staring at him in puzzlement. The opponent was taller by only a few inches but solid and mean. As the victor of the previous two fights, he was primed and ready for a real fight. He looked disappointed as the little one got to the center.

To get the fight over with so a better fighter could come in, he sent his fist down towards the little one's head. And missed. His fist slammed into the stone floor and his head followed, creating a physical and sonic crack. The little one was sailing backwards into the air and landed on the outer edge of the arena. His eyes were wide with fright, instinct having taken over in the split second he defended himself.

When the downed fighter didn't move, the enforcer declared the little one the victor. That meant he would fight in the last battle of the night. The Chancellor's hands shook with trepidation. In shock he turned to the Count who also had the same reaction on his face.

"What was that?" Count Ambrook demanded. "Where did this one come from?"

"I am having him analyzed, my lord."

"How much strength does he have?"

"Actually, he is only fed twice a day because he's greedy."

Count Ambrook's eyes opened wider.

"That is on near starvation? Why haven't you reported this to me?"

"You seldom come to these fights and I assumed you would wait until the final rounds to see the outcome. As small as he is, I figured he would lose eventually."

"I have no doubt that he will not. Bring me the details of your findings and tell no one."

"As you wish, my lord."

The two men continued to watch the last fight and as his master predicted, the little one was the victor. Another defeat in one blow.

Chancellor Rayne swiveled in his chair eyeing the stack of papers that detailed the results of the little fighter's DNA. The information was shocking for its lack of what was missing. Nothing extraordinary jumped out of the reports signifying some rhyme or reason to the boy's strength. At the end of the selection battle, he was the one still able to get to his feet. The other four had to be carried out.

A tap on his door broke his attention and he turned his chair towards it. Count Ambrook stood leaning against the frame, a serious expression on his face.

"You have the results, I see."

"I would have come to you, my lord."

Count Ambrook waved the notion away and sat across from him. He perused the report then tossed it back down.

"This tells us nothing!" He sat back in disgust.

"No, but it does show an enormous appetite for someone so young of small stature. There are very few vampires with that kind of feeding requirement."

"Yes, most of them are ancient." The Chancellor folded his hands.

"Yes."

Both vampires locked eyes and they had no need to speak. When they broke their gaze, Count Ambrook leaned forward.

"What do you think he is?"

"I can't tell. We have to observe him for a good length of time."

"We can't feed him like that. It would raise suspicion."

"My thoughts exactly. I will keep him on a rationed diet of three meals a day."

"Where is he now?"

"Getting cleaned up for your son. Since he is also a gender shifter, we think it best to let them connect that way."

Count Ambrook stood up and glanced back at him.

"Well, that just killed two birds with one stone."

"Let's hope his guardian can keep him occupied more than less."

ANNOUNCEMENTS

Selections were done but the work was not over yet. Count Ambrook leaned back in his chair and let the blood rush in his head. There was now a period of assimilation for the guardians and children chosen for the project. He knew his son would rebel and did not relish the confrontation. A meeting had to be set up with all the coven leaders to get the last minute preparations in order. They had all the time in the world but he preferred it get done within the next few years. His wife entered the room and rubbed his shoulders.

Relaxing into it, he let his head rest on her bosom. Times like these were few and far between.

"You work too hard."

"I want it done right."

"He'll be angry."

"This is a good thing for him."

"Oh, I agree."

"This is more like a summit," Count Marchand exclaimed while settling into his designated seat at the front of the table for his coven.

Elegantly embossed name placards were place in the center of each table represented by all eight. The large conference room had been rented out three months in advance and accommodated nicely. Well worth it so far.

Along with the eight main covens, the twelve lower ones were also attending. This school involved all vampires in the region. Noncompliance was not an option. A few of the lower houses had protested in the beginning but after a reconnaissance of their offspring, they quickly changed their tune.

"Yes, well, we should have done this long ago." Queen Erena slid into her seat and readjusted her dress after crossing her legs. "Who is facilitating this tonight?"

"Why, Count Ambrook, of course. We can't let him out of the spotlight just yet."

"Shame on you all for forcing him into handling the planning."

"I didn't see you object, Queen Erena," Count Marchand sneered.

They exchanged blood red glares then focused their attention on watching the rest of the coven heads arrive.

Count Ambrook sighed in frustration. Did they forget that he could hear them? Seeing the other seven coven leaders dismiss him as some sort of servant almost made him angry until he remembered his coven was one of the high three. As the one who did most of the planning, he also had the most power when it came to important decisions. His wife took his hand under the table and rubbed the outside of his thumb. Relaxing, he too decided to people watch.

The lower houses' attire made him cringe. They were not leading by example, not by a long shot. Sloppy, trendy and gaudy. It ran the gambit and was in great contrast to the eight main covens. The worst culprit was the seventh house with their take on new Gothic. Like something out of a bad B rated vampire movie from the late twentieth century. He saw Queen Erena and Queen Celeste tilt their heads towards them to have a look and their faces scrunched up as if smelling something rotten. Count Sapienti shook his head with distaste.

When everyone was seated, Count Ambrook raised the gavel next to him and banged it three times. The conversations ceased and the attendees' focused on the front of the room.

"Thank you for coming. Let's begin, shall we? As you know, a plan to re-educate our young on our culture and history was set in motion. I am delighted to inform you that it is now a reality." A few claps were heard. "Each of you have contributed by finding individuals knowledgeable about your coven to fill the instructor positions. I extend my gratitude."

"And now?" Count Grieger of the seventh house leaned back in his chair indignant.

"Now, we refine our resources and prepare our children for transport in the coming years."

"How do you propose we 'spring' this news on them?" Count Sapienti stood and turned to face Count Grieger.

"Who runs your coven? You or your offspring? That is a non- issue. They obey or pay the consequences."

A few of the coven leaders squirmed in their seats, embarrassed by the question and offended by Count Sapienti's response.

"We have a few years before the finalized curriculums and this gives them a chance to get used to having a guardian at all times."

"And the neutral zone? Are we supposed to let our children go and hope there are no incidents?"

"The last time I checked, our children were capable of hunting and killing. They are by no means helpless. Unless," Queen Celeste paused, "YOUR children have not been trained to defend themselves after all these decades." She raised a hand to her lips and preened.

Fangs and hisses filled the room from the lower covens and Count Ambrook leaned back in his seat and contemplated letting the brawl happen. This was not going as planned. "It's the nursery pen of 1885," Count Marchand whispered to his accountant.

"Yes," the accountant replied. "But they are supposed to know better."

Hearing that, Count Ambrook stood from his table and banged the gravel.

"Enough!" Everyone turned their attention to him. "And you wonder why our offspring behaves as they do? This!"

"Maybe we should all take courses at our new school." Count Marchand puffed his chest.

Falson hurriedly put his clothes back on, panic thumping through him. The messenger was quite clear on the timeline. His father requested his presence in ten minutes which meant he had to scale the walls outside and reenter as close to the throne room without being detected by enforcers. The servant girl lay on the floor half naked sobbing from his at- tempted assault now rudely interrupted.

"Get up! And do not let anyone see you leave."

He climbed out of his window and gauged the distance of his destination.

"I can make it."

With two minutes to spare, he arrived in the corridor of his father's throne room, proudly strutting in at his accomplishment. Inside were the entire council and their oldest children. A sense of dread crept in as he stood with the other four offspring. His father's gaze drilled into him like hot embers.

"Since the five of you have a tendency to disobey your elders, we have decided a guardian should be with you at all times. They will report to us when summoned and make sure you comply with our demands."

"A babysitter?" Falson yelled out. "You must be joking!" "I will not be insulted like this. Father!" The head enforcer's daughter looked towards him.

"Silence!"

Count Sapienti's voice rang in their ears, the high pitched after tone forcing them to their knees. Blood seeped out of their ears through their fingers and their faces stared up in agony at the ceiling. When it faded, all five were on the floor panting.

"I will not tolerate your behavior any longer. None of us will. You will do as instructed."

His enforcer looked down on them.

"Your guardians will be assigned to you within a few days. I suggest you think about how you are going to adjust to your newfound situation."

"Dismissed." His father commanded.

He picked himself off the floor and staggered out of the throne room, his equilibrium still a bit off from the ringing in his ears. The walk to his chamber seemed longer than normal. Once in his room, he flopped down on the bed and yelled into the covers. Getting a guardian, a tattle tale, to watch his every move pissed him off. That was for children, adolescents. He was nearly sixty years old. Young in vampire years, yes, but no less a man.

He had a feeling it would surely be some sniveling servant from the lower class. A thought came to him and he lifted his head up.

Maybe I can persuade my new pet to do MY bidding instead of my father's.

He had no intention of changing his lifestyle because his father forbade it.

If there was one thing Princess Adelia despised it was being handled like a child and told to obey. Thus, when her mother informed her that she would be assigned a guardian, she threw a tantrum in the throne room. The other four, apparently in the same boat, stood staring at her in complete awe. She swore and spit and hissed and screamed. In her moment of rebellion, she had forgotten who and what her mother was.

Her mother reminded her swiftly.

With superhuman speed, the Queen came down from her throne and black talons plunged through Adelia's ribcage. She spit up blood and her eyes locked with her mother's blood red ones. Disgust, rage. Pink saliva dribble from her mother's mouth, the long fangs extended.

Oh God! She's going to kill me!

Adelia whimpered, a silent plea for forgiveness. It worked. The Queen ripped her talons from her body and let her drop to the floor in a bloody heap.

"Get her out of here. I do not wish to see her until the time is near."

Until the time is near? What did that mean?

"The rest of you need to remember your place. Be gone."

The same two enforcers from before grabbed Adelia by the arms and dragged her out into the hall. From there, she was picked up by the doctor and taken to the infirmary. The whole way she told herself over and over, *BE smarter!*

Dawn was still an hour away but Chase, Chase, forced his small entourage to follow him back to the castle. Over the past two years, he had noticed shadows constantly nearby every time he went out for a little fun with his friends. Tonight was a bust. They had gotten drunk, ended up in a fight with some humans who could care less that they were vampires and almost got killed. A group of people were coming out of the side door of a movie theatre so they ambushed them and got to feeding only to abandon ship when screaming from some passersby started. Nothing was ever reported as far as he knew but it was obvious someone was keeping tabs.

Nearing the side entrance of the castle he stopped short. The doors had been sealed shut. He looked back at his friends and they too were taken aback. There were only two ways in; scale the walls to his bedroom window or through the front gates. A quick scan of the walls and to his window found it too had been sealed. When he turned to ask for suggestions, six enforcers came around the bend heading straight for them.

"Dude," his childhood friend said, "something ain't right."

The leader of the enforcers came up to him.

"Your father requests your presence immediately. Post haste if you please. Dawn is near."

"My friends?"

"Will be escorted to their rooms."

Chase sighed heavily and followed the enforcer. He could tell something really was off for his father to go to such lengths. As he entered the castle, the high council members frowned then went ahead of him into his father's throne room. Standing next to his parents was Chancellor Rayne. He halted his conversation with them to turn and give him a dirty look.

"I see you made it back before sunrise, yet again." His father's voice had a sharp edge.

"Just out and about. Lost track of time."

He noticed the council members' children were also present and glanced over at them. Not one turned to acknowledge him. They actually looked scared.

"Yes, so I've heard."

I knew it! So someone has been reporting on my endeavors. "Since you all seem to have a knack for going out and creating havoc wherever you go, we have decided to have someone with you at all times. A personal watcher who will report to me."

"You mean a nursemaid," he son snapped.

"Tread carefully," his mother sneered, leaning forward. He had not seen her like that in decades and never towards him. This was serious.

"I haven't done anything to warrant such a decision."

"Oh? Did you not attack a random group of people on more than one occasion? Did you not put the lives of your friends and yourself in danger by antagonizing humans in the district?"

He clamped his mouth shut and balled his fists. What did it matter? Humans were nothing to be afraid of and no one cared about those old vampire tales anymore.

"It's the twenty first century. We need to get with the times, Father."

The other four finally turned to look at him and there was anger.

"I have done some stupid things like you have but I do respect our culture. Some laws shouldn't be broken," the Chancellor's son said.

"This is bullshit!" A council member's daughter shouted.

Her father went over and cracked her across the face with the back of his hand.

"You will comply! Dawn is near."

His father waved them away and they all exited the room. In the hallway, he seethed with contempt for whoever reported him. Then he wondered what kind of sap would be attached to him. He had seen some of the other servants that waited on his friends hand and foot. Early on he opted not to have that. Now he had no choice.

Back in his room, he unsealed his window and drew the drapes closed, enveloping the room in pitch darkness. As he stripped naked and climbed into bed he realized he had forgot to ask when the nursemaid plan was going into effect. Laying there thinking about it, he figured bending the person to his will would be the quickest way to continue his nightly rituals.

Taps came from his door and he sat up contemplating if he should open it. No doubt it was one of his female friends looking to share his bed before the sun came to interrupt. Another tap. He decided against it, knowing his father's minions were probably eavesdropping. He heard footsteps leaving and laid back down, suddenly exhausted.

TWO: COVEN ELITE

AMBROOK COVEN

The moment he stepped into the room, he could smell her. His cock hardened, straining against the crotch of his pants. She lay unconscious on the lounge seat, naked. Her matted light brown hair clung to her pristine face boasting soft slightly parted full lips. He stood frozen, mesmerized, vaguely aware of his father's butler removing his boots and clothes. As his manhood was freed, springing upright in a slight curve, a drop of bloody pre-cum fell from the tip.

"We found a servant for you in the lower halls. She's not exactly of the purest blood and is capable of shifting gender. I think this one is perfect for your needs." Chase's eyes began to sting, a signal they were turning red. "All you have to do now is make her yours."

He climbed onto her, spreading her legs with his knees as he entered her. His hands slid in position beneath her shoulders. He went deeper inside as he leaned forward and his back muscles tightened. Lush euphoria seized him and his head fell back, a soft sigh revealing long sharp fangs. He sank them into the crook of her neck.

A whimpering intake of breath followed by her body shuddering under his weight was too much for him to endure. His thrusts became long and hard as he drank the sweetest blood he had ever tasted. Like fine aged wine, its flavor permeated every cell within him. Her body resisted for a brief moment then relented. He fell into a drunken state, relishing the feel of her skin, her scent; her taste.

His fingernails grew, piercing the fabric of the cushions as he released his seed. Covered in sweat, he slowly retracted his fangs and licked the puncture wounds. His saliva seeped down inside sealing them shut. Sitting upright forced his softened cock to worm its way out of her womb and slither across her lower half, leaving a sticky wet trail before resting at the crease of her thigh. He inhaled deep, his eyes fluttering shut while the blood lingered in his mouth.

Making a small slit on his wrist with a talon, he let his own blood trickle into hers. When it seemed to be enough, he clamped his hand on the cut to stop the flow before licking it closed.

"Very good, sir."

His father's butler came into his side view and produced a wet cloth which he used to wipe the mess away. A strangled cry escaped the female's lips and her body arched high above the lounge seat, another louder scream of anguish unleashed. He moved to hold her down, help her, but the butler stopped him.

"No, you must let it run its course through her system. Come." The butler put his shirt on for him and pulled him off the cushioned seat by the elbow. "Finish getting dressed and go rest. I will have her brought to your chamber, later."

Reluctant to leave but knowing the butler was right, he pulled his pants back on. Not bothering with his boots, he left, making his way to the court-yard for some fresh air.

There on his bed, she lay sleeping. Her breathing seemed labored, her skin flushed in a golden hue.

So pretty. Yet, I have to treat her like a slave.

He knew that's not what his father called his new guardian but that is what this creature was. Someone who would cater to his whims but obligated like all the other slaves to tell the leader of the coven when things were not up to par.

His cock twitched, threatening to bulge out of the leggings he wore as he watched her naked body roll over on its side. While they were out in public or doing duties in the castle, she would be in male form. But if he wished for sex when they were alone, he would have his new pet anyway he wanted, male or female.

He crawled onto the bed and laid next to her so they were face to face. Her warm breath smelled like she tasted and he couldn't help but lean over and brush his lips against hers. It wasn't supposed to happen this way. The guardian would show up, he would get the blood pact over with and go about his usual routine. This was a huge monkey wrench because he knew he could never let her go.

SAPIENTI COVEN

A knock on Falson's door woke him and he checked the clock above. He had slept through the day hours and it was again night. That alarmed him. Sitting up quickly proved a bad idea and he remembered the confrontation with his father a few nights before, the effects still lingering. The knock came again.

"Enter!" Yelling hurt his head.

The door opened and a young vampire was shoved into the room, landing halfway between it and the bed. His father's councilman stood in the doorway.

"You need to make a blood pact with him. When you're done, your father is having an assembly within the hour." With that, he left, shutting the door behind him.

Falson looked down at the young man on his floor and hissed in disgust. He had to exchange fluids with someone like that? It was clear the man was from the lower levels and had no sense of etiquette. Still on the floor, he made no at- tempt to show respect for his new master.

"How dare you come in here and not acknowledge me." The fighter, now guardian, stared up at him with disinterest which made him angrier. "You will obey me!"

He leaned back to sit on his knees and blew a lock of hair from his face.

"You have not requested anything."

Falson jumped from the bed and grabbed him by the hair, pulling his head back to expose the neck. He could see the carotid artery pulsing. Without notice, he bit down hard squirting blood onto his shirt. To his amazement, it tasted good. Better than good, it was intoxicating. He almost went too far, the young man's body going limp his cue. On the night stand was a small dagger he used for target practice. Using it to slice his own wrist, he let the blood flow into the fighter's mouth.

The clock clicked over to the next hour, startling him and he realized the assembly time was near. Where had the time gone? He patted his guardian on the cheeks a few times until he opened his eyes.

"Stop slacking off. We have a meeting with my father. Get to your feet."

Glassy eyed and disoriented, his guardian made a few attempts to do so and was finally able to half stand. Falson caught him before he fell back down and started to convulse.

Shit! I drank too much.

The little bit he gave back was not enough to put him to normal levels and he was sure his father would see this. Desperate for a plan, he came up with one on the fly.

"Bite." He held out his arm to the guardian once the fits ceased. When he felt teeth sink in, he said, "Now, walk with me. Don't stop until we get to the throne halls."

They hurried out of his bedroom, his guardian's mouth attached to his arm as they walked. He did not want another incident with his father like before.

During the assembly, he half listened to his father's spiel while keeping an eye on his new charge. Of course, it was to be the other way around. The man's gaze seemed out of sorts but at some point a clarity came and he stood straighter. Relieved, Falson took a deep breath. The other young vampires stuck with guardians looked put out by the events as he did. When they were all dismissed, the tension was high.

Back in his bed chamber, he saw that a bed was set up on the far end of his room so he pushed his guardian towards it and watched him land hard on the mattress. A sense of guilt tugged at him but he shook it off.

"You're not going to tell my father anything that I don't want you to, is that clear?"

"That's not how this works," his guardian whispered back.

"What did you say?" He went over and grabbed him by the chin. "You belong to me and you will do as I tell you." He shoved him down again.

"I am not afraid of you like I am of your father."

He stopped his walk to his dresser and clenched his fists. That was true. Even he was afraid of his father to some degree, knowing the man would never kill him. He hoped anyway.

"Regardless! Do we have an understanding?"

A quick glance over his shoulder and he saw his guardian reposition himself on the bed for comfort.

"Sure."

His soft voice sent a shiver through him and he could hear the blood flowing in his veins. A hard on stirred in his pants as he remembered how that blood lingered on his taste buds. He was partial to women but for this case in particular, he could swing the other way. His glance turned into a scanning of the man's body and found it of ample flesh. Not scrawny but well-built with the right amount of meat. His guardian had fallen asleep which was a good thing because he needed to recharge. Falson had no doubt that his hunger would resurface later on and this time he had to restrain himself.

Falson's guardian woke up to giggles coming from the other side of the room. A quick rundown of the previous days made him remember where he was. It didn't surprise him that hours after receiving a guardian, the prince was on track doing his usual rendezvous. His vision focused on the female standing in the middle of the room flirting with the prince who sat leaned back on the bed in a come hither sort of pose.

Disgusting. And disrespectful to the Count.

He judged the female as someone from a lower coven because her manner of dress was old fashioned from the last two centuries. Her hair was fairly long and not quite blond. Lifting his head up off the pillow he cleared his throat.

"I do not believe this is good judgement on your part, my lord."

Both prince and whore turned to him with looks of anger.

"How dare you speak to me, servant!"

The female's voice grated on his ears.

"It is not your place to interfere with my endeavors." His ward spat.

"If it is in the castle of my master, it does."

"Do you not know how to keep your slaves in place?"

The whore gave a crooked smile.

"I just acquired this one," the prince answered.

She sped over and cracked him across the face with the back of her hand. The ends of her talons grazed his cheek, leaving fresh thin blood lines. Satisfied, she returned to the bed and stripped off her dress. She climbed on top of the prince and helped him out of his clothes. They wrestled and laughed while engaging in fornication right in front of him. At one point the prince and he locked eyes. The prince immediately averted his eyes in what seemed like embarrassment.

As you should be.

He laid back down and turned over so he couldn't see any more of it, waiting until he heard the finishing cries of orgasm from her. Giggling still, she didn't understand the prince's urgency to be rid of her as he rolled over and watched the prince toss her off the bed.

"Get dressed. You need to leave."

"Of course. We don't want you to get in trouble with Daddy." She glanced over at him.

The prince's face grew dark but he didn't move from the bed. The female picked her dress off the floor and pulled it back on. Her boots were solid leather so she had no need to lace them up like most female vampires did.

"Just leave." The guardian sat up ruffling his hair.

She came at him and was ready to strike but the prince grabbed her by the wrist and yanked her back. Startled, she was about to protest, when the prince shoved her out of the door and slammed it shut. Naked in the middle of the chamber he turned to him with glowing red eyes and a semi erection.

Before he could react, the prince was on him, his fangs sinking deep into his flesh. He drank greedily and the guardian began to feel faint within moments. His limbs went slack and the prince's embrace tightened, drawing him closer. Without warning, the prince wrenched himself off and staggered away from the bed. His breathing was fast and heavy and blood smeared the lower half of his face. Some of it dripped down onto his chest and formed bright lines that traveled to his navel.

Wiping his face with the back of his arm and hand before using his palm, he walked backwards to the bathroom and shut the door. Bleeding from his wound, the guardian thought for the second time that he was going to die before fulfilling his duties. The bathroom door banged open and the prince came running out.

"Shit!" He covered the wound with his mouth and used his saliva to coat it. The sting was as bad as the bite. Fully slathered, the prince removed his lips from him. "Shit, shit, shit!"

The blood congealed and the flow stopped. He looked over at the prince and felt a pang of pity for the young vampire.

"I'm sorry. I forgot to stop."

His remorse was short lived as he became angry at, who? The Prince pushed him away and returned to the bathroom, leaving him to recover alone. The guardian decided to stop the prince himself if necessary. He didn't fight his way out of the slums to become food. His duties were clear but he would give the prince some leeway. If at any time the reputation of the coven was in peril, he would pull the reins on him. Exhausted, he fell asleep.

DE LUCE COVEN

The Lieutenant's son made a silent declaration. It had been the longest five days of his life. He actually slept for an entire day which brought suspicion that he may have been drugged. After that, he was confined and fed four meals a day. There was absolutely nothing to do in his small stone cell with no windows and a small iron grate at the top of the door. Finally, on the last day, he was taken out of his cell and hosed down like a prison inmate against the side walls. Two guards grabbed his naked body by the armpits and literally dragged him up the stairs to another room on the fourth level.

Inside the room was a seamstress and a groomer. They went to work measuring every inch of him and then left him there. He took a look around and saw the frilly pillows, silk ribbons and knee high lace up boots.

Oh fuck!

He knew immediately whose room it was and cringed at the thought of forming a blood pact with the spoiled demented princess. The Queen said he would be her guardian but he knew better than that. Reining in the princess was a hard task for anyone. Not one to shuck his duties, he vowed to do his best. One thing was for sure, he would not put up with her drama or sexual advances. He had no desire for her whatsoever, contrary to what she thought of every male in the vicinity.

The door flung open and the devil herself stood staring ferociously at him, all anger and rage. She did a jump step right at him, her talons ready to close around his neck. He dodged her advance by stepping to one side. Her body sailed right past him and slammed into the bed. Her face planted into the covers while her legs, splayed like scissors, went high up in the air before landing on the mattress with feet dangling over the edge.

He pulled his lips in and tried to stifle his laughter. It was the most undignified thing he had ever seen and felt lucky to have witnessed the almighty Princess Adelia accomplish it. Her head popped up in mere seconds and she turned red eyed at him. She hissed loudly, her fangs dripping with saliva. Crawling on all fours she moved as a spider would to rotate her body so she could be dead center in front of him.

This is bad.

A degenerate? Yes. Spoiled rotten? Of course. But, she was a princess with the Queen's blood running through her veins which meant power. Before he could speak to calm her down, she leapt at him with incredible speed and her wide-open mouth clamped down on his neck like a vice. He had never had fangs so painful inflict his flesh and she was not gentle, as if she were trying to tear his throat out. So excruciating the pain, he blacked out.

The sound of banging and yelling made him force his eyes open. In the haze, he saw tall women in battle armor holding the princess by her pretty blond hair while she kicked and screamed, blood everywhere. A hand on his neck caused him to flinch and he turned to see whose it was. Another enforcer had sealed his wound though some blood seeped out from the edges of her palm. His hearing returned full blast.

"He's mine to do what I please!"

The princess strained to get at him. Her eyes bulged out of their sockets in madness and hunger.

"They said to make him mine! I can do what I want!"

"We're losing him," the enforcer next to him said.

She was right. He could feel his consciousness leaving him again, his vision fading.

That bitch.

Red light burned his retinas yet it hurt to move his eyes let alone open his eyelids. The loud thumping in his ears was validation that his blood pumped strong in his arteries. He somehow got his arms to move and rested them on his chest.

"Get up!"

This time he forced his eyes to open and tilted his head towards the angry voice. He found himself on a bed on the other side of the princess' room and cursed his luck. He would have to live in this room with her as well. She sat on her knees on the bed with fists digging into the covers. Her hair was immaculate and she wore a dress only someone of wholesome attributes could pull off.

"Mother is waiting," she snapped.

He licked his lips and winced at the sandpaper swipe across cracked skin.

"I need clothes first." His voice sounded harsh.

A sinister smile spread on her face as she stared down at his partially limp dick. She waited and when nothing happened, she frowned. He smiled to himself. Obviously disappointed, she climbed off the bed and went to the settee. A pile of neatly folded clothes sat on top along with boots and his sword underneath. She tossed the clothes at him, ruining the perfect set.

He slowly got dressed then walked over to retrieve his gear. Running a hand through his hair he sighed. The Princess marched out of the room and stopped in the hallway.

"You're mine now. You must obey me. Let's go."

He followed her down the corridor and up two more levels until they reached the opened doors of the Queen's throne room. Her entire council was present as were the other four fighters he had defeated. They stood next to the children of what appeared to be high class coven members. Princess Adelia shoved her way to be front and center, a show of superiority in her mind he guessed.

"Good. You are all here." The Queen relaxed in her seat and draped an arm across her lap. "I wanted to formally thank you and welcome you into my circle. I can tell you that it will not be an easy task but it will be greatly rewarded."

She nodded towards her head councilman who stepped down to them.

"There will be a banquet held at midnight for you. Please get more acquainted with each other and enjoy the festivities."

The looks on both offspring and guardians' faces spoke volumes of rebellion and resentment.

"You are dismissed."

"You stay, daughter. And your guardian."

He was given looks of pity as the others walked out, the general's son shrugging at him. When only they remained in front of Queen and council, she came down from her throne and lifted the princess off the ground by her neck.

"A guardian protects you. A guardian risks his life for you. YOU, do not try to drain or maim him for your own sick pleasure. He is yours, bound by blood. But make no mistake, he answers to ME!"

The Queen dropped her daughter as a fainting woman did a handkerchief in the old days. He nodded in approval and bowed low in respect for his master.

"Now, you are dismissed. Take her away from here."

He grabbed the princess by the arm and hauled her up on both feet. Still dazed, she wobbled a bit when walking. He tried to keep her steady until she got her balance and angrily yanked her arm from his grip. It was almost comical, the situation he found himself in.

In Adelia's bed chamber she continued to steam, muttering about humans until she noticed him standing by the door. She had forgotten he was there. That weird look graced her porcelain mug of a face and she smiled.

"Undress me, slave," she spat.

He didn't move except to fold his arms.

"I am not your slave, Princess. Or did you not understand my duties as our Queen dictated?"

Her eyes glowed and she hissed. Sighing, he unfolded his arms and went to stand behind her. She smirked and turned her head forward, waiting. He twirled the tip of the string at the end of her corset for a moment then yanked it, hard, placing his foot on her back to push her forward.

The corset flew off her and she flew onto the bed in that undignified way as before. This time, he did laugh out loud. In an instant, she was within an inch from him but so was his sword drawn between them and it stopped her cold. She searched his face and the edge of the blade in quick succession, thinking.

"I am your guardian but make no mistake, I am also a servant of the Queen and she is who I fear. I'll let you do what you want. To a degree. The role of the coven and its status must be maintained. Are we clear?"

"How dare," she started.

He pushed her back and stepped away from her in a defensive stance. Her head cocked to one side and then she gave up, crawling onto her bed in defeat. His sword sheathed, he went to his own bed and plopped down.

"How about I make you feel better?"

Her voice had a hint of honey but the undertone made him cringe. He turned his head and saw her shirt undone with her hands squeezing her breasts. The visual alone was sad to him but he grinned and leaned back.

"Those clammy fingers on my flesh while you grunt and feed on me like some animal would not make me feel better. I respectfully decline."

She screamed in rage.

That didn't go well.

Fearing she might come back at him, he gripped his sword. To his amazement, the windows flew open and off she went, wings extended. He ran to the ledge and watched her sail downward then arc up. She hovered for a bit then shot out towards the city. He climbed onto the window sill and grimaced. To have to chase her so early on was not his idea of getting acquainted. Jumping down, he too made his way in her direction. In her state of mind, he had a feeling she would hunt.

Not good.

THREE: SCHOOL LIFE

REBELLION

The multi-coven school of re-education was a huge collection of buildings spanning nearly a two mile radius. The main entrance courtyard could accommodate over thirty vehicles if needed with large spaces for buses. For the first tour of the facility, that is what happened. Every coven leader came with their chosen's parents to see how their money was spent on the interior. Not so much extravagant but at the least a comfortable environment for their ungrateful children.

Count Ambrook, Count Sapienti and Queen Erena stood at the forefront of the gates while they waited for the custodian to open them. After three and a half years, their vision was complete. Many of the instructors and others working within the school were still moving in, getting settled in the housing complex. The next phase would be to get the students in.

Behind them, a row of vehicles sat with their engines running. Count Ambrook didn't glance over to take a count but he knew all of them had come. The custodian, an old vampire hunched over with long grey stringy hair, came to enter the code that released the gate's mechanism. Queen Erena raised an eyebrow at him.

"Really, Count Ambrook?"

"Nostalgia?" He replied.

The old vampire was a like a movie relic, stereotypical of the humans' idea of them. There were some who resembled that but they were only half vampires, hence the aged appearance. Despite that, these beings had the strength of ten men so were often underestimated.

"I like it," Count Sapienti laughed.

They moved forward to the main entrance while the vehicles came rolling through the gates and parked to let out their occupants. On the top of the stairs, the three coven leaders turned to face the crowd.

"Welcome to our school of knowledge dedicated to our kind." Queen Erena raised her arms in victory. "Let us revel in our joint success."

With that, Count Sapienti pushed open the double doors.

Renovations had been a pain in the ass, the structure essentially decrepit. The walls were falling apart on the inside and out forcing them to fork out money for bricklayers and demolition men. It was worth the effort because every floor looked beautiful. Each classroom was uniform in size and decor, the halls wide enough to let six people walk across in comfort. The combination of dark wood floors and light wooded walls gave it a modern yet old world feel.

Count Ambrook watched the horde of vampires ooh and ahh at everything. He felt a new kind of relief, the knots in his gut unwinding. Queen Erena patted him on the back of his shoulder. She too had reservations about how the hordes would perceive the school. Onward to the housing complex and even he was surprised.

Being a boarding school, the rooms were dormitory style with two beds, a desk and a private bathroom. Nothing fancy, but humbling to say the least. Count Echols' wife let out a small laugh.

"Our little rodent will have a fit. No expensive decor or wine. I can hear his rants already."

"I believe they will all feel that way. Especially since they will live here during school sessions and be at home for breaks and holidays," Count Sapienti interjected.

"So, it really is like a true school?" Queen Celeste asked. "Full accreditation and all," Count Ambrook replied.

Nods and murmurs of approval went around the corridors.

"Now all we have to do is drag them here and make them comply."

"The announcements should be made at the same time so we can coordinate intake days."

"Agreed. Say in two weeks' time?"

Ambrook Coven

Chase Ambrook threw one of his books at the wall in anger and yelled at it. He grabbed a handful of his hair, pacing the floor. His head throbbed.

School!

He had never been to school ever because there was no need. He had learned all he needed to know from books, and going out into the world. To be treated like some human teenager and forced into an institute of education smacked of hate in his mind. A jealousy against the younger generation. And a boarding school at that. His guardian was supposed to make sure his studies were completed or they would 'face consequences'.

His guardian never said a word as usual. He was mostly quiet and soft spoken, submitting to his brutal assaults, sexual or otherwise. While he and his father engaged in a yelling match, his guardian stood still looking down at the floor. When they left the throne room, he said one thing.

"You shouldn't do that."

Thus, the moment they returned to their bedroom, he grabbed him by the neck and bit down. Engrossed in his feeding, he ripped out the back of the guardian's pants and forced his erection in. The young vampire didn't struggle so he pulled him closer and they fell onto his bed. His eyes glazed over with ecstasy and he almost went too far, again.

Satiated, he had redressed and continued his displays of anger by throwing things. He picked up a heavy box from his shelf and chucked it. It was caught midair by his guardian who was now awake. In the throes of his embrace, the young vampire had shifted gender and sat naked, the sheet falling away to expose all of her.

Fuck, she's so damn pretty.

The tightness in his groin threatened to take over so he started doing breathing techniques which calmed it and him down.

"It's not so bad," she spoke.

He turned to her and smiled.

"Really? Have you ever been to school?" She shook her head. "I have seen movies, read books and even encountered some of these schools. They're dins of hormones, cruelty and," he stopped.

Unlike humans he felt vampires had a better handle on those things. Nonetheless, he didn't like being thrown into such an environment even if only vampires were attending.

"Get dressed. We have to start packing."

Watching her crawl out of bed to the closet he stifled his urge to take her one more time. She had become an ad- diction so he treated her with sadistic cruelty to counter it. In such close quarters as a dorm room, he feared it may get worse.

Sapienti Coven

"How awful!" The lower house princess exclaimed in a pouty voice while wrapped around Falson.

This was the third time in a year he had bedded her and it now had no sense of excitement. He told her about the whole school thing in hopes of getting some sort of sympathy but she laughed it off. The last remark, turned his erection soft and he sat up.

"You should go," his guardian said to her.

Her face scrunched up as she retrieved her dress and he in turn put his clothes back on while still in bed. As he had one knee on the bed and a foot on the floor, she went over to his guardian and grabbed him by the hair.

"You fucking slave! You need to learn your place and keep your mouth shut!"

Her grip tightened and she kept him steady as her fist slammed into the side of his head.

In the same instance, his bedroom door opened.

"Is this how you let others treat those in the circle of the Count?"

His father's enforcer stood in the doorway with two others behind him and his insides flipped. The female let go of his guardian and stepped back in defiance.

"He's only a slave. Who cares?"

No.

Falson went over and pushed her towards the door. One of the enforcers took hold of her and dragged her off screaming in protest down the hall.

"This is what you do to the one who is bound to protect you in the neutral zone? Has this been how he treats you all this time?"

"I was about to handle the situation before you came in," he said before his guardian could answer.

It hit him like a two ton weight as to why he was given a guardian and ordered to 'acquaint' himself. He had been told constantly by his father and his guardian that he was not a slave or a servant. The enforcer frowned, not believing him and stepped further into the room. Falson walked over to his guardian and inspected the bruise forming on his face.

"Are you alright?"

Steely eyes returned his and he flinched. Only fair that his guardian was angry. To the enforcer, he tilted his head while holding his guardian's against his chest.

"Why are you here?"

"To inform you of your new home's space restraints and to pack accordingly."

"Yeah, I got that. You can leave now."

As the two enforcers left, he looked down on his guardian and caressed his hair.

"I'm sorry."

"You always are."

His guardian leaned closer to him and they sat like that for a while.

De Luce Coven

Lariod, Adelia's guardian, tried to keep up with the princess' pace as she hauled ass down the corridor towards the staircase that lead to their chamber. As usual, she was upset about the Queen's decisions, this one even he worried about. Bad enough they resided in the same room in the castle but a dormitory was a quarter of the size and he may have to commit Royalcide (his term for killing your monarchy).

In her hurried state, he noticed her hips swaying wildly with her fervent stride. He rolled his eyes. It never ceased. Along the walls stood soldiers in from sentry duty and he could already imagine the look on her face. Her sashaying had started the moment they rounded the corner.

"Such dishonesty! She should have told me what this whole guardian plan of hers was for in the first place. I don't need teaching." Her voice was an octave higher than normal, making her sound more feminine. IT didn't fool him at all. She abruptly stopped and whirled around on him. "Did you know? She told you, didn't she?" Blood red eyes searched his.

"No, Princess, she did not. I too am vexed by this new information."

She turned back around, her hair whipping him in the face. He glanced up at the ceiling in exasperation and continued to follow as she resumed her insane pace. Only a few of the soldiers gave her a second look and he chided them silently.

Don't be stupid.

The expressions the men she bedded had on their face as they exited her chamber was one of confusion? Disbelief? And now he would have to deal with her going after fellow schoolmates. Great. At the door to their room she pushed it open forcibly causing it to bang against the wall. She stood in the entrance, one hand holding the door fast to the wall and scanned the interior.

"I want my dresses packed in a sealed case and my human clothes in boxes."

"Why are you telling me this? Call your servants."

He walked in past her and sat on his bed. She didn't move from her position but her face had turned pink. That's a lot of blood flow. Then she yelled like a banshee, letting the door go, and came at him. For a moment, he contemplated if he should meet her head on and push her back or dodge. When her talons extended, he made up his mind and rolled away. She reared back at the last minute and stumbled backwards without falling.

Ahh, she learned.

"Keep still!"

"You must be joking," he said.

An enforcer came in and cleared her throat. Adelia turned her upper body towards her.

"What do you want?"

Uh Oh.

The enforcer had her hand around the Princess' neck in a flash and lifted her so they were eye to eye. No red eyes needed, the enforcer's icy blue ones conveyed enough malice that even the Princess could understand.

"I am not your pet. You will show me the respect I have earned."

The Princess was dropped like a sack of meal. He controlled his urge to laugh but a slight slip came out. Regaining his composure, he sat silently while the Princess picked herself up off the floor.

"I am her to tell you that there will be no servants to help you. You will take minimal provisions and leave this castle in the transport provided with your guardian. Is that clear?"

He had a feeling that would be the case. By the sounds of it, there would be uniforms issued. The enforcer turned to him and he knew what she was going to say next.

"Your weapons will remain in a safe house on the outer premises. None are allowed on school grounds."

"Just fangs and talons," he quipped.

"Correct."

She pivoted towards the door and left as stealthily as she came. The Princess frowned and wiped the snot from her nose with the back of her hand.

"Fucking slave. I should have her killed."

Lariod looked over at her in disbelief. Of course she would show bravado after the Queen's enforcer leaves but that remark alone could get her killed. Shaking his head, he stood up and came within a few inches of her.

"Adelia," he made sure his tone was authoritative, "this is not up for debate. You will comply with the Queen's decree. Now, let's get packed and take our leave."

"If your blood wasn't so awful tasting, I'd drain you," she seethed.

"That's your reason?"

She fell backwards onto the edge of her bed and parted her legs.

"You're just mad you can't have me. I'll keep it a secret, if you like."

He sighed and walked away from her.

"I'd rather have my throat torn out by a pack of werewolves than bed you for even a second."

That did it.

She crashed into him, her weight that of a tank belying her size. Her fangs chomped down on him and she started to feed as if hunger had consumed her. Right before he passed out, she let go, spitting the residue out onto the floor.

"Don't you ever say that to me again! You deserved that."

His last thought was, *"Would the Queen miss her if she died?*

The sleek forty foot luxury bus pulled into the courtyard of the school, its brakes hissing as it made a full stop. Night was in its deepest hour, the sky pitch black making the stars look like jewels. Chase sat with his head against the window staring at them in wonder. Inside the vehicle was loud. The other students were still cursing and throwing tantrums from the time they boarded. A small brush of hair on his neck made him look over at his guardian, Baltise, sitting next to him. He was asleep and had slid towards him when the bus stopped.

His gaze zeroed in on those perfect pink lips, slightly parted, warm sweet breath blowing into his face. He wanted to kiss him. Remembering his sur-roundings, he fought that feeling and gently shook him awake. Red eyes greeted him and he panicked for a moment before digging into the bag at his feet to bring out a chunk of cured meat.

"Eat this, now," he whispered.

Baltise took it, devouring it in mere seconds but the red faded to his normal eye color and Chase breathed in relief. No one needed to know how much his guardian ate. Three vampires stood on the top steps of the school entrance waiting for everyone to debark. Baltise picked up their two satchels and let him pass as did the other guardians for their charges.

The female vampire in the middle of the three held a clipboard in one hand and a menacing stare. She wore a wine colored skirt suit with a white shirt and her dark hair hung in waves across one shoulder. From his research over the decades he knew that she was the Dean of the school. He gauged her age at around 500 give or take which meant she was not inclined to tolerate disobedience. They would all have to tread carefully.

As they stepped out of the vehicle, a giant of a man bellowed at them.

"Line it up! Single file straight across so we can get a good look at you scum."

Chase saw Queen Erena's daughter open her mouth to say something and her guardian clamped his hand over it. The giant enforcer heard the smack and turned his attention to them as her guardian removed his hand.

"Something to say, Princess?"

The way he elongated princess made it clear he was not going to take her crap. Her status meant nothing here. When she didn't reply, he averted his gaze and resumed walking in front of them for inspection.

Disciplinarian.

He stopped in front of Chase and sniffed.

"Count Ambrook's pretty little boy. Just because he spearheaded this project and did most of the planning doesn't give you any privileges."

He could feel the others' stares on him and knew the man had done this on purpose. Better yet, he wasn't lying either. Rage built up inside him and was easily extinguished when Baltise's hand brushed against his.

"Move out!"

At first no one moved, not understanding, until the giant man grabbed one of the students and tossed him to the bottom of the stairs. The Dean looked down on him in disgust.

"State your name and guardian."

The student, dazed and hurt, was barely able to raise his head. Blood trickled into his left eye. His guardian was there in a flash to help him up and gave the Dean what she wanted. Everyone nearly ran towards the steps for fear of being treated like the first guy. They formed a single file line one after the other and slowly made their way inside, the doors swinging open to welcome them.

Hell on Earth.

That is what Chase thought before going in to see for himself. He was sure the others felt the same way.

Falson did a slow walk through the small room and his hands balled into fists. It wasn't the size that bothered him, he couldn't care less. It was the thinness of the walls. He wouldn't hear someone clearly but even muffled it can get irritating over time. Plus, he didn't want anyone hearing what he might be doing in his own room. There was no fear of that in the castle.

Demitri dropped their luggage at his feet as he sat on the bed on the adjacent wall and leaned his head against it. The bed sitting in the middle between the two windows was Falson's. A night stand on each side and a dresser a few feet away. Next to Demitri's bed was the study desk with two chairs and a bookshelf. He went into the bathroom and was surprised to find a soaker tub with shower head above. Two sinks, a medicine cabinet and a toilet rounded it out.

Back in the room, he halted at the sight of his guardian sitting cross-legged on the bed, eyes closed and head resting on the wall. His chest thumped hard and his groin tightened. He squeezed his hands and his eyes shut forcing his body to behave. The smell of Demitri's blood wafted in his nose and from where he stood could see the jugular vein pulsing.

A thud and loud voices muffled by the walls snapped him out of his state and he cursed himself for almost losing it. Instead, he went over and caressed Demitri's forehead, moving stray hairs out of the way. He had taken him more than a few times over the few years they'd known each other and its intoxicating effects still lingered. Still, he told himself that he loved female flesh and didn't swing the other way.

"What are you doing?" Demitri's voice startled him.

"Being nice to you for a little while."

His eyes opened and they stared at one another. "Just don't," he let out a small breath.

"I know. I'm not feeding off you today, so stop being childish."

A banging on their door made them both look at it in confusion. It stopped for a second then came again. He got up and opened it. Princess Adelia stood hands on hips with a smirk on her face.

"We're on the same floor." She said with a devious smile.

Oh, hell no.

He stepped back from the door and caught her guardian's stare conveying the same thing. There was pity in that look as well.

Princess Adelia had only seen Falson from afar at parties or around town so she was delighted to finally see him up close and was not disappointed. He was every bit as gorgeous as she had heard from some of the other princesses he had bedded. In an attempt to at least put herself on his to do list, she decided to introduce herself as soon as they dropped off their bags.

While he stood there in long shirt and leggings, she assessed his package. Her mouth went downward and she nodded in somewhat approval. Not bad. Off to his right was his guardian and she sucked in air through her teeth. Jealousy reared. How dare he have such a beautiful guardian when she had to deal with, she turned her head slightly towards hers. He seemed amused.

"So, Falson Sapienti, what say you and I have a little fun while we're incarcerated in this place? No need for it to be dull, hmm?"

His guardian was between them in the blink of an eye.

"You need to leave."

The door slammed shut in her face. Stunned, she blinked a few times. Her hands fell from her hips and she had her foot up ready to kick the door in when a heavy presence came near her. Menacing and dark, leaving her in mid stance as she turned to see where it was coming from.

Dean Valencia stood not five feet away from her, an aura of death surrounding her as her eyes glowed silver. Princess Adelia slowly lowered her leg and set her foot back down on the ground. Lariod stepped in next to her in a defensive stance, his demeanor showing malice.

"Adelia De Luce. I see we have a problem day one." The Dean cut her gaze to her guardian. "Stand down, or face the consequences."

"You know I cannot do that if your intent is to harm my charge."

"Oh, I haven't done anything yet. Keep your pet on a leash in my school."

The Dean turned away, writing something on her clipboard as she walked off.

"Humph," Adelia said. "She has some nerve coming at me like that. Addressing me like a commoner, too. I commend you on doing your job." She turned to smile at him and her face faltered.

The look he gave her was one of disgust, shame and anger. His eyes glowed for a brief second then he too walked off back to their room. Tears threatened to sting her eyes but she fought them back. There was no reason for her to feel this way from that. Defeated for now, she followed suit.

Feeling the deadly aura even in the safety of their room, Falson and Demitri had backed all the way to the window in case all hell broke loose. Intruded on by the Princess was shocking enough, but the Dean proved to be an enemy not to mess with. They knew it was her because she oozed malice at their first encounter. When the heavy darkness lifted, they sat on the bed.

Falson realized he had been holding his breath and let it out. He also saw that he had been holding on to his guardian's hands. He let go of one hand and pull him close, kissing him deeply. Satisfied, he disengaged.

"That was quite rude of you to slam the door in the Princess' face."

A dark and sinister look clouded his guardian's face.

"Stay away from that animal. She smells of blood."

He laughed.

"We all do."

"Human blood."

That took him by surprise. He had heard rumors that she had a knack for kidnapping and torturing humans but determined that's all they were. Demitri had been to the other castles for meetings and had probably confirmed it. Putting that aside, it was not why he despised her. She had a nasty personality and the rumors didn't help her case. The way she scanned his body like a piece of meat let him know what was on her mind and he would rather have hot coals raked across his back than bed her. Regardless of how pretty she was which was a shame. Disappointing even.

Feeling agitated, he pushed his guardian face down on the bed and pulled his leggings off then his own.

"I want you," he breathed in Demitri's ear as he forced his way inside him. "Don't fight me. I'll hurt you."

He felt his body relax beneath him. So much better. The bed covers stifled his guardian's cries but he still glanced up nervous that someone might be near, listening.

The cafeteria had a mix of cooked human food and raw meat. Chase wondered if the meat was fresh. All the stu- dents filed in and went through the food line, their guardians grabbing what they wanted and placing it on their trays. He let Baltise take one slab of raw meat and the rest fruits and vegetables. He had no taste for much of anything but knew he had to eat something.

A quiet storm was brewing amongst the students, their situation solidifying a growing dissent. He didn't blame them for he felt the same. As long as they didn't comply, the elders would eventually realize this was all for naught and shut it down. That was the consensus so far. He figured six months, maybe a year into this and they would all be back at the castle doing whatever they wanted again.

That said, the facility was very well done. He could get used to the whole cafeteria idea. It eliminated his need to sneak food for his guardian. From what the pamphlet stated it was to be open from dusk until dawn every day.

The instructor caught every one's attention and he peered at them one by one, anger permeating from his body. He had asked a question from the homework and no one had raised their hand to answer.

"Not one of you?"

Some of the students smirked while others remained preoccupied with extracurricular activities. The blatant disrespect for the instructor's authority was rampant.

"You!" He pointed to Falson.

"Not a clue. Not interested." He didn't even look up from the book he was reading which was not the one for class.

"Your guardian knows the answer." He addressed him. "Don't you?"

"Yes, I do," Demitri answered.

The bell signaling the end of class and a fifteen minute reprieve for getting to the next rang out. Everyone fled out of the classroom jovial. Chase grinned as he left and Princess Adelia let out a hearty laugh as she flirted with another student. The instructor glared at them all.

Chase tossed his books on the floor and flopped down on the bed. He had taken the two beds and made one, giving the room more space in the middle. Whenever there was an inspection though, he returned it to its original set up. Baltise sat down at the study desk and laid out notepad, books and pen. That made him angry. Everyone's guardian was doing the work and trying to force their masters to study. Even his had not given up on the ritual.

At last break back at the castle, his father's councilmen and even the Chancellor would ask him history questions in the halls. When he didn't answer correctly or refused, they would ask his guardian. If he got it right, they were allowed to pass. So far, there were no signs of his father or the other coven leaders backing down from their schooling agenda. He wasn't sure what it would take to end it.

"Come over here," he commanded.

His guardian gave him a hurt look that made him angrier.

"Now!"

Setting down the pen, Baltise went to him and sat on the bed. He pulled him down and sank his fangs into his shoulder, letting the euphoria take him. The guardian struggled beneath him for a bit then went slack. For a moment he thought something was wrong until he felt the slight movement of his body trying to relax. He tried not to be so rough but it never happened that way. Loud noises from the hall- way brought him out his happy place and he suspended his feeding for now.

That was the one thing he didn't like about the housing complex. Too many people in close prox- imity of each other. Baltise shuddered beneath him and he forgot how cold he got sometimes afterward. Wrenching the blanket free from the top, he wrapped it around him tight. He sat up and wiped the excess blood from his mouth with two fingers and went to the door.

On the other side was an ominous presence and he waited to decipher who it may be before opening it. Confirming it was not the Dean, he swung the door open to reveal Princess Adelia's guardian. He was bigger than him by a good three to four inches with a lot more muscle.

"What brings you here?"

"This little stint of yours and the others will go badly."

"I have no idea what you're talking about."

The guardian planted himself like a root to the floor and folded his arms across his chest.

"Do you know what I did before becoming that brat's guardian?"

"No idea."

"I was in the guard. My father was a lieutenant and that is how I was chosen as a candidate."

Chase felt his smile fade. He had assumed all this time that every guardian had been picked from the slums or the servants in the lower class. This bode ill.

"Is that so?"

"We guardians are under the service of the coven leaders, not any of you. This blockade, if you will, is going to hurt all of us."

With that, the guardian turned and left. Chase stood in the doorway feeling a sense of fear for the first time since the start of it all.

What had I not planned on?

Dean Valencia walked the halls of the education center and took note of the guardians clambering up the ladders in the library while their charges lounged in the commune as if nothing was wrong. Over the past eight months she had gone through a ream of paper on her clipboard, detailing every student's action for her reports to the coven leaders.

Princess Adelia was the worst offender, refusing to adhere to boundary rules by sneaking out at night to hunt in the neutral zone. Luckily, the enforcers on staff were able to snatch her back to the fold before she was noticed, let alone had grabbed some human who may have turned out to be a vampire slayer. Her guardian had long ago stopped trying to subdue her and knew there would be punishment for that.

She didn't blame him. HE valued his life as much as the others, the princess having no such conviction thinking herself invincible. Out of the corner of her vision she glimpsed Chase, the mastermind of this asinine rebellion, perusing the shelves in the lounge for a book. He seemed carefree as usual but there was an underlying of something else.

Had he realized his fatal flaw in planning? It was the one thing that was reiterated repeatedly yet every student merely glossed over it, continuing their behavior. They would learn soon enough after the next break.

PUNISHMENT

Falson stepped out of the shiny black Bentley his father had sent for him at the school and on to the platform of his castle. It was good to be home again even if only for a week. Demitri came up behind him and stretched while yawning loudly. The servants hurried to the trunk and retrieved their bags then literally ran into the castle. That was odd.

As he walked in, he noticed the time was a little after ten, giving him time to change into his regular clothes and rest before his father's midnight rally of the coven. In every hallway he encountered nervous looks and some of the elders even tsked at him. He assumed why. They probably felt he should be benefitting from all the schooling. It's not that he didn't catch on to some things, he just didn't see the purpose or care.

Back in their bed chamber, he and his guardian stripped off their uniforms and went to the closet for more comfortable digs. Wanting to feel regal for a change, Falson chose leather pants, a silk shirt and waist coat of dark blue. He tossed a pair of leggings, white shirt and maroon vest at Demitri. Their boots had been polished recently and sat at the edge of his bed.

Better dressed, admiring himself in the full length mirror, he made a nod and sat at the dresser. In the mirror, he watched his guardian crawl onto his own bed and curl up like a baby. He was not very cheerful to begin with, but there was a deeper anxiety hanging over the man. Maybe after the coven meeting, he could try to make him feel better.

On the way to the assembly room, his father's right hand enforcer came up to him, blocking their path. He stared down at him with a sneer. His guardian actually backed away instead of shielding him.

"So, young master. What have you learned about our clan's origin these past few weeks?"

This again. Every time they came back on a break it was the game of twenty questions.

"What exactly are you wanting to know?"

"Oh, the year of our first castle built."

"We only have one castle and this is it. If you're going to play games, at least be fair."

The enforcer grinned and turned back to where he came from, heading to the meeting.

"That was stupidity on his part, don't you think?"

He turned to Demitri and was taken aback by the vampire's look of defeat. When their eyes met, a burning rage is what he found. Dismissing it, he continued down the hall to his father's throne room. As they neared it, many of the vampires were leaving and it was not yet midnight. None looked his way. The flow became a flood the closer he got and at the entryway he saw only the high council and the elders left in his father's presence.

"What's going on?" He demanded.

His focus landed on the splatter of blood in the center of the room and then the other classmates from his coven slack in the arms of their parents' servants. An enforcer grabbed his guardian and a fight ensued as he struggled to get out of their clutches. He went to stop them and he too was grabbed and held back by his father's men.

"What's the meaning of this?"

He exposed his fangs and hissed. His guardian was stripped naked and his wrists tied together by a rope which was then pulled until he dangled in midair. Directly above the still wet bloodwork below. Frightened, he fought harder to get to his guardian but the enforcers held fast to him.

"What was the question asked?" His father turned to the enforcer from the hall earlier.

"The year of our first castle."

"Ah, yes. Such turbulent times. Did he answer?"

"He insisted that this was the only castle in our clan" The history instructor was led in and brought before Count Sapienti.

"When did you teach this information, Lord Instructor?"

"Three weeks ago, my lord."

"So it would be fresh in my son's mind then?"

"That is to be assumed, yes."

"Thank you. You may step back."

The history instructor bowed and went to stand against the wall with the other elders.

Falson strained with every fiber of his being to get away, his eyes never wavering from Demitri's body hanging like a chandelier. Yes, he vaguely remembered a topic in class about the different clans and their early years, but why was that so important?

"Guardian!" Demitri's fingers twitched. "What year did we build our first castle?"

"1582," was the whispered response.

His father leaned further back in his seat, getting more comfortable.

"I brought all of you here to witness what happens when you do not answer correctly. Every time you fail this test, your guardian suffers the consequences. They know what is in store for them when you all come home, ignorant and defiant. Your fellow classmates have already been shown this." With a nod to his enforcers, the two men each produced heavy ten-foot cat of nine tails. Sharp razor tips glistened at the ends of each.

"No! No, no, no! Don't do this!"

In practiced unison, the enforcers struck his guardian with the whips, tearing flesh that wept red rivers. The sound of his guardian's cries as the enforcers drew back in quick succession to release more blows made his body go weak and he knew why the others were non-communicative laying slackened on the floor. Bloody tears blurred his vision and he clenched his teeth, a guttural animal sound emitting from his throat.

Unable to stand it, he let out a yell and grew talons. He was able to get away from his captors for only a few seconds before they got him back and this time, he could not budge. Helpless, he stood straighter, not giving them or his father the satisfaction of seeing him fall apart. He would not be some weak master like the others. His gaze didn't waver from his guardian.

When it was over, his father staring at him in curiosity, the rope was lowered and the medical team came to whisk his guardian away. He could feel his eyes burning and knew they were glowing bright red. He wrenched his arms from the enforcers' grip and continued to stand.

"See you next break." His father's smile was terrifying to most but he only felt rage. "Take them out of here and have this mess cleaned so the coven won't get distracted during the meeting."

The moment he returned to his chamber, he screamed and unleashed a series of blows to the wall. Caved in pieces crumbled to the floor as he held his head in his hands. Tears fell onto the leather pants and slid down slowly into the creases around his knees, never hitting the floor. So distraught that all the energy drained from him and he fell asleep in that position.

The door opening.

He heard its slow creak which only happened when someone was trying to be quiet. Muted candlelight from the corridor seeped around the silhouettes of the dark figures entering his room. With stiffness restricting his movements, he turned his head slightly. The first figure deposited a large bundle on his guardian's bed and then the two left, closing the door to engulf the room in darkness yet again.

It didn't take long for his eyes to adjust and see Demitri laying on the top of the bed covers, unmoving. He forced his body to move, shaking off the body aches and went to him. Straining from the weight, he picked him up and carried him over to his bed. They went falling into the bed together, his guardian like dead weight. The clock showed 4 am. Dawn was coming. He stripped both of their clothes off. Only the top cover was heavy so he used it to wrap them in.

"I'm so sorry," he whispered.

Forgive me.

It was so loud in his head that he realized it may have been sent telepathically. As proof, he heard a soft reply in his mind.

You always are.

De Luce Coven

Princess Adelia stood bored at the congregation of elders in her mother's throne room. As usual, she had been bombarded with some silly questions that she should have been taught the answer to in school. Her coven classmates were all bent out of shape over something, weepy and scared. There was blood everywhere and it made her giddy with pleasure and disappointment that she wasn't a part of the festivities. Lariod was unusually quiet and she assumed he wasn't used to that level of bloodletting.

"Time to pay the consequences for my daughter's lack of resolve."

The Queen addressed her guardian and she watched him slowly walk to the middle of the room. He removed his clothes and let the enforcers bind his wrists. As he was raised up like a rack of beef, she cocked her head in confusion.

"For your charge to not know the same information as you is a failure on your part. It has also come to my attention that you have let her escape the premises with no effort to stop her."

"As he should. I am not some child to keep on a leash," she spouted. "Just because he wants to learn all that dull stuff doesn't mean I have to."

Hateful looks came from her coven classmates and she frowned. Not wanting to know why, she continued.

"Do I get to punish him? Are we using the bullwhip?"

In her excitement, she failed to assess the situation until she looked around again and saw that no one was cracking a smile. She suddenly felt a sense of dread as she once again sought her mother's eyes and then her guardian's. He hung there in silence, awaiting whatever was to come.

"If she moves even an inch, restrain her. If she struggles, incapacitate her."

"What?"

Before she could ask anymore, the two amazon enforcers did indeed pull out bullwhips and immediately began assaulting her guardian relentlessly. He stifled his yells through gritted teeth but they still echoed in the chamber. Adelia was rooted where she stood in a state of despair. She had no idea what to do, her mind going a mile a minute on scenarios where she tries to negotiate with her mother.

There were always jokes about doing him in or torturing him, but she wasn't being serious. He had not been protecting her lately and now she had an answer as to why. Why should he defend someone like her who had no regard for his life as he saw it? The blood of her guardian mingled with the rest of the splatter on the floor and she figured out where the pools of red came from.

So that's what happened.

The last crack of a whip followed by silence pulled her out of her reverie. Her vision came back full force and she saw that some of her guardian's blood had flew onto her dress creating speckles of color on the white blouse not covered by her corset.

"Why?" She heard herself ask.

"For every question you do not answer, this is the outcome. Did you think they were there for your enjoyment? Pets? They are accountable for your education as well as your safety."

"Drop him," her mother's head enforcer commanded.

Adelia tensed with anger and stayed in place as Lariod was let loose to fall in a heap on the slick floor.

"Take your guardians and leave."

Princess Adelia saw the others slowly rise to their feet and turn to the unmoving bodies of their guardians behind them. Their parents who had stood restraining them moved out of the way. She looked over at Lariod and shuddered. He was twice her size and probably weighed a ton in his current state. So many humans were tortured by her hands yet she couldn't bear to see her guardian covered in blood from wounds inflicted by someone else.

"This is wrong, what you're doing. He has done nothing to be punished in this way." She got her arms under his and pulled slowly towards the entrance.

"Did you not offer to do it yourself, daughter?"

The daughter part was said like acid and hurt as much. Fighting back tears as she hauled off her guardian, she stared her mother in the face.

"I was being facetious. Mother."

The Queen lifted off her throne and two enforcers caught her before she reached the bottom of its base. Adelia's eyes grew wide and she hastened her exit with guardian in tow. The others were already ahead of her, their guardians nowhere near the size of hers. She had gone too far; she could feel it. A rift had opened between mother and daughter and she was no longer protected. That being said, she would not let anyone know she was heartbroken. She would continue to act like always, no matter how much damage it caused.

Ambrook Coven

It took five enforcers to hold Chase at bay while his guardian screamed as the other enforcers stripped off her clothes. They had forced her into female form and laughed at her smallness. On the throne, his father sat unfazed, having done this to the other classmates' guardians already.

"Don't you touch her! Stop!" She was raised up like cattle. "God damn you!"

That made his father sit up.

"Me? We have all been damned long ago. This is your doing."

The spiked tassels of the whip made a clinking sound as the enforcer reared back and let it fly towards Baltise. Her blood curdling screams incited his own and the room sounded like a house of horrors. At one point, he managed to nearly decapitate one of the enforcers holding him and rip- ping the intestines out of another. His father made a motion with his hand and four more enforcers tackled him a mere four feet from her, her blood dripping down on him in globs before he was dragged back and held tight. They had him by the arms arched backwards forcing him to look up.

Count Ambrook saw the desperation and insanity in his son's eyes and held up a hand to cease the punishment. The screaming was more than even he could take and the tiny vampire looked pitiful hanging above. His son had saliva dribbling from his mouth, eyes blood red with the promise of death and every vein visible bulged. This may have been a bit too much to be shown to the offspring but it had been the course decided after no improvement of the situation.

"You forgot the one thing we said at the beginning of all this. Your guardians are in service to us for your sake. Yet, you all insist on treating them like playthings or slaves in your misguided minds. This has been going on the whole time but none of you noticed. What does that say about your treatment of them?"

As the rope was released, letting Baltise's body fall to the floor, he leapt from his throne and caught her in both arms. He gently laid her down and stepped away.

"Take her for treatment," he said to the medical officer standing by. "And make sure my enforcers are well taken care of as well." His son was still seething, eyes streaming tears for his guardian. "Let him go when she's away from here."

He sat back down on his throne and thanked the heavens his wife was not here to witness this. She would have put a stop to it the moment the guardian started screaming. She did not need to know this part of the plan. By doing this, he hoped his son would stop the little coup he started and take his schooling more seriously. There was more at stake than any of them knew.

Once the room was cleared, the enforcers let his son go and he fell forward on his knees. His talons scraped the tile as saliva and tears mingled forming a pool under him. With labored breathing he slammed a fist into the floor and let out a primal yell.

"Good. You're angry." He listened to his son cry for as long as he could stand. "Take him to his chamber. Clean him up."

His enforcers bowed and carried his son off.

"I am sorry, my son."

He rested his head on his hand as he leaned on the arm- rest of his throne. Chancellor Rayne came up beside him and they both watched the boy slumped in defeat leave against his own accord.

Heavy. Like lead bricks.

That's how his body felt as he regained conscious-ness. His eyes would not yet open but he could hear the soft hum of activity outside his bedchamber which meant the door was open. A presence hov-ered above him and then a dark figure blackened the muted light behind his eyes.

"He's coming around. The mental exhaustion was hard on him."

"Let's give him another day," he heard the Chancellor's voice say.

A sharp prick on his arm was followed by a slip back into the deep darkness.

He bolted upright in his bed, having difficulty breathing and clutched his chest. His hair was drenched with sweat and he used his other hand to wipe the sticky strands from his face. The memories of his guardian's torture flooded into him and he rocked back and forth, determined not to yell in frustration. As he was about to slam his fist into the bed covers next to him, he stopped. Below his closed hand, Baltise lay sleeping. A pained expression was etched on her pretty face.

Careful not to disturb her, he slid back down and nestled closer to her. He could feel the heat of her body and her blood smelled bitter. There wasn't enough circulating through. He would have to feed her a lot before their return to the school. His own blood felt hot. Knowing that this is what had been going on all this time, made him ill. Adelia's guardian had warned him and the two things clicked.

The rebellion was over. He would make sure of that. Some of the students didn't care but he did and to never have his guardian endure such a travesty again was all that mattered. He was sure Falson felt the same. Adelia on the other hand, he wasn't sure. With gently fingers, he caressed Baltise's forehead then kissed her lips.

No more defiance. Is what he told himself.

APT PUPILS

Dean Valencia noticed the change almost immediately as the students came off the bus in silence. There were a few still attempting to show strength while the rest knew what had to be done. Chase stepped off and managed a sly smile at her before commanding his guardian to move onward. She smiled back even though he had already focused his attention elsewhere.

Let's see how this term goes.

Adelia pushed her way past Lariod and entered their dorm room first. She did a quick inspection to make sure nothing had been taken during the break and satisfied, plopped on her bed. Lariod tossed their bags on the floor by the door and did the same. He threw one arm across his eyes and let out a sigh but the deepness of it had her cringing in anger.

"Now that we're back from my mother's comedy hour, we can get back to doing what I want."

Her guardian's body went still and from beneath his arm she saw his steely gaze of hate. Not acknowledging her remark, he rolled over so that he couldn't see her. She knew he was angry and her words were not nice, but she couldn't back down.

"Oh come on. It's not like she was going to kill you. Let's get some food from the cafeteria and start over, hmm?"

"I am not in the mood for eating."

"Whether you're in the mood or not is irrelevant. You need to eat. Come."

She slid off the bed and went to the door. He didn't move. With high speed, she came to hover above him, fangs extended.

"Now!"

He rolled onto his back and stared at her for a moment. Then he sat up and waited for her to move. When she did and returned to the door, he obediently followed. Relieved, she continued into the hallway.

"I think you should get a few chunks of raw meat to start off. I'm in the mood for a hearty soup if they have it."

As she rambled on about the food choices in the cafeteria she periodically glanced back at him. He would never want her; that was certain now. But she could at least try to get him to want to protect her again. In the cafeteria, she let him go first, which was unusual for her and made him stall for a bit. She cursed herself but it was too late.

The cafeteria was nearly full and almost every guardian was eating the raw meat which was understandable considering some had recently woken from deep slumber. Their wounds were so severe that they had to be put in coffins and sealed. That alone left a bad taste in their masters' mouths.

Dean Valencia surveyed the students and watched the consumption of fruits and vegetables in addition to the raw meat. At least they were eating a balanced diet. It would do no one any good if they all fell apart from something like this.

Chase sat quietly watching his guardian eat a massive amount of food. Such greed. He himself barely ate a thing. His eyes were still a bit swollen from his outbursts during the torture. She had heard about it and found the account much more brutal than the others. Of course, hearing what Princess Adelia had said during her guardian's punishment was no surprise and she loathed the girl even more.

Falson was also quiet but there was a different kind of resolve in his expression. As if it had nothing to do with the school. Seeing everyone doing okay, she left the cafeteria to get ready for tomorrow's lessons. A recap of the past term was in order.

Not even a month had gone by and he was already too far gone to stop. Chase grabbed Baltise by the hair as he closed their room door and shoved him onto the double bed. He climbed on top of him and ripped his shirt from the shoulder. Sinking his fangs deep he felt the intoxicating rush of flavorful blood fill his mouth and he drank greedily. His body settled down onto his guardian's and the feeling of longing took over. On the verge of tears.

Without meaning to, he said telepathically, "I can't let you go."

It startled him realizing he had done that but not enough to stop him from feeding. In answer, Baltise ran fingers through his hair.

He disengaged and licked the wounds clean, his acidic saliva sealing them and they healed in mere moments. When he sat up, he saw his guardian's eyes were red. Shit! He had taken too much.

"Hungry," Baltise whispered.

"I know. I'll feed you, I promise."

He kissed him hard and was about to stop but surrendered to his lust. In desperation, he stripped their clothes and flipped him over, shoving his cock deep inside. If anyone came knocking, he wouldn't answer and definitely wouldn't stop. Baltise was his addiction and no one was going to take that away. His guardian let out a sharp cry as he thrust hard and he could tell that one had hurt. He slowed his rhythm and felt him relax a little.

Sure enough, as he climaxed, spewing his seed, there was a knock on their door. Disgusted at being interrupted even though he was done, he pulled his pants back on and went to see who had dared to do so.

Falson stood in the doorway, his guardian standing behind him with his back to them. The two monarch offspring stared each other down for a brief moment, assessing the other's strength.

"What can I do for you?"

Falson's gaze traveled to the bed and Chase blocked his view.

"I came to see what other ingenious plan you may have in store and to let you know I will not be participating."

"No need to worry. There is none. I think we should comply to the best of our abilities."

"Hmm." His stare moved to behind him again and his mouth opened in shock. "Are you screwing your guardian?" Revelation glinted on his face.

"Are you?" He replied accusingly.

Falson backed away, the playful shock removed from him. Chase shut the door on him and went back to his bed.

"There's a saying about glass houses," Demitri stated.

"I know the saying," he snapped.

"Is that really all you wanted to know?"

"In a sense, yes. His plan of rebellion nearly got all of our guardians killed."

"No one forced you to go along with it."

His guardian walked ahead of him back to their dorm room leaving him standing in stunned humiliation. That was true. He was too old to go around blaming others for his actions. The reason for the school crept in his mind and he concluded that the elders may be right. They indeed had become blood-sucking brats with no real dignified way of living.

Back in their room he accosted his guardian with the one question he had never asked.

"Where were you chosen from? What did you do before becoming my guardian?"

"I lived in the slums below the castle and fought in the cage for food and status."

"What?" Falson blinked a few times then sat down. "What do you mean, the slums below the castle?"

His guardian looked at him as if he were jesting.

"Below the castle. Where the lower class resides."

"No, the lower class lives in the slums on the out-skirts of the town."

"Those are the ones who won fights to get status outside of the castle."

"These fights. You say they are in a cage?"

"Yes."

"In the slums below the castle?"

"Actually, it's in a cavern between the slums and the lower class. Since it is underground, the fighters can go back and forth."

"For what?"

"When you win a fight, you have to keep winning to keep your status. If you lose, then you are back in the slums or at the very least, declassed."

"I have never heard of such a thing!"

"I thought everyone in the higher class knew since many of them come down to see the fights on occasion."

Falson went pale.

"You're lying. How can you justify telling something so vicious about our coven?"

Demitri gave him a strange look then shrugged.

"Believe whatever you want. I know what I had to do in order to eat and stay under a roof of my own."

"My father is not a tyrant!"

"If that's what you want me to say, then so be it. He is not a tyrant."

He backhanded his guardian without thinking and regretted it the instant he did.

"I," he said.

Demitri got up and opened the door, turning to him once before leaving with the door open. Falson slid down to the floor hurt and in shock. This was not how the conversation was supposed to go. He only wanted to know about his guardian and learned more than he bargained for.

Class was wrapping up and the instructor waited until everyone had packed up their things before clearing his throat to get their attention. His students halted their activity and turned to him.

"Just to let you know, I will be giving a test on this subject at the end of the week. I don't need to reiterate its importance."

Angry looks and slack jawed indignation followed his announcement. He smiled at them, nodding as they passed his desk when the bell rang. Even with that warning, he wondered how many would actually study, having learned their lesson about noncompliance. Some of the leaders' offspring really didn't give a damn and it showed in their work. Outside his classroom, the Dean waited patiently for him. They nodded in greeting and fell in step with each other as they walked down the hall to the staff meeting room. It was time for the monthly report so they could pool their notes together for the elders. He was eager to find out what the other instructors encountered since the punishments became known.

A seat was vacant at the far end of the table so he took it while the Dean sat at the head, placing her clipboard beside her. She took out a pair of wire rimmed glasses and set them on her face as if they were a delicate item.

"Let's begin. At the end of this session our History Instructor will make an assessment and give recommendations."

The staff opened their own notepads and waited their turn to give a report.

Chase strolled through the halls whistling a catchy tune and his guardian followed behind him with a sullen look. Baltise had suggested they go to the library and gather study materials but he declined and they went to the gaming room instead. After an hour there, he made his way to the cafeteria for a snack, forcing his guardian to eat something as well.

As they entered their dorm room, Baltise set down their books and bit his lower lip before speaking.

"If we get all the notes done in the next hour or two we can go over them tomorrow."

"I'm going to take a nap then see what's going on in the commons later on."

"Then I could start on the first two subjects and..."

He didn't let him finish. Giving him a hopeful glance he told him.

"Baltise. Trust me."

He watched the distrust linger in his guardian's eyes. Saying so was not a guarantee he would do as asked. Sighing, he ran his fingers in his guardian's hair then pulled him close. The only way to gain his trust was to prove it. Kissing him on the head, he went to his bed and laid down. He fell asleep almost instantly.

When he woke, more than a couple of hours had past. It was fully dark outside at 3 am and he could hear the going ons in the commons. His guardian lay next to him deep in slumber and that disturbed him. He should be awake. Sitting up he caught a glance at the desk and saw the neat stacks of books and notepads.

He went over and sat at the desk. Opening the notebook in front of him he found the notes for the test in perfect form, separated out for an optimal study guide. A cracking sound made him flinch and he had a flashback of his guardian being tortured. He had no idea what was happening in the commons but he knew then that he would not be going.

Making himself comfortable, he started reading the notes and memorizing the key points. Dawn crept in before he knew it and he hurried over to shutter the windows. Baltise had not stirred. Was something wrong with him? Sleeping through the night was not normal vampire behavior. Tired, he made a mental note to take him to the nurse's office before class then crawled back into bed.

Studying was not Falson's forte but he endured it for the sake of his guardian and his own sanity. The revelation he had some weeks ago stemming from his guardian's story left him in a state of madness. It shouldn't have surprised him, vampires being known for various forms of debauchery, but he assumed his coven was more sophisticated than that by the way his father ran the classes. During the history lessons, he learned even more about his coven in particular and wanted to retch then and there.

The subject of the test was along the lines of the pacts between covens and humans from a century ago. He remembered that time because he was so elated to be able to mingle and hunt freely without causing alarm. Looking back on it, he saw it now as the decline of the vampires' power. Each pact, or treaty, held something that had pros and cons for both sides.

His guardian sat on his bed leaning against the wall taking a much needed nap. They had compiled many notes and it took nearly two hours to organize them. He reached for a book and another fell off the desk and onto the floor with a loud bang, waking Demitri.

The vampire opened his eyes and turned his head to him.

"I didn't mean to wake you."

"It's fine. How far have you gotten?"

He raised up and slid into the chair next to him.

"About halfway. This is hard."

Falson tapped his pen on the desk then tossed it against the wall. It bounced back to him, rolling along the edge.

"I trust you."

Demitri leaned his head on his shoulder and closed his eyes. Falson stared at that beautiful face for longer than he intended. Minutes ticked by until he forced his gaze away.

"Focus," his guardian said.

Not realizing he had not been asleep startled him and he nearly fell out of his chair save for Demitri catching him midway. Back upright, he leaned over and kissed him. And again, deeper, more fervently. Between kisses, his guardian tried to pull away.

"Falson," he managed finally.

He gave him one more kiss before doing as told, focusing on the notes.

"I know," he said in frustration.

His pants were tight at the crotch from his erection and he knew if he succumbed to his desires right now, he would not get his studying done. That came with dire consequences he wanted no part of.

"Let go of me!"

Princess Adelia's guardian did so and she went flying into his desired destination; the chair in front of the desk. Her little ass went down hard on the wooden seat and she jumped back up to try getting to the door again. This time, he grabbed her in a bear hug and plopped her down in it. She struggled for a bit then locked eyes, giving him a dirty look.

"I will do it later," she sneered.

"No. You do it now. Just because you enjoy seeing me tortured doesn't mean I like it."

Her face took on a new expression he wasn't sure he liked. It sent mixed signals.

"Whatever. There's no reason for me to do it right this second. There's a party in the commons and I'm going." She smiled slyly at him. "Unless you've decided to submit to me and I don't have to look for fun elsewhere."

He bared his teeth in disgust and pushed off her. His insides felt like they had flipped over.

"Fine. I'm not going with you."

"You have to!"

The last thing he wanted to do was watch her in action as she tried to seduce some random man into her bed. Her eyes roamed the commons the second they entered the place and he kept a safe distance. At first, he felt sorry for the victims but then decided they deserved their punishment. Finding one she liked, the princess signaled it was time to leave the party. All he had to do was keep the Dean off their backs since the princess was under more scrutiny than the others.

He waited in the hallway outside their room while she entertained her lay of the month. Though muffled, he could hear the grunting and whimpering from inside. It went on for nearly half an hour and when it stopped he thank the merciful Gods. A few students had come through the halls during the deed and gave strange glances his way.

The door opened and a young count from the lower fifth clan shuffled into the doorway. His stare was empty, fixated on nothing as his head hung a bit low. Noticing Lariod, he made a quick glance to him.

He had seen that look so many times. Confusion and disbelief. Shaking his head in pity for the man's sake, he watched him proceed past him. His guard- ian was down the hall and came hurrying to him, perplexed by his master's state.

Lariod pushed himself off the wall and turned into the room. It was a mess. Sheets were strewn over the bed, the pillows on the floor and a stench lingered in the air. Blood, cum and sweat. One look at the princess sitting naked on her knees, thighs spread wide open and a triumphant face he backed out.

"I am not coming back in here until you clean this up."

"What?"

She started to crawl off the bed so he hastened his way to the door.

"And when you're done, we study."

He was able to shut the door on her when she got within a few feet of him. Bile came up and he forced it back down long enough to get to the communal bathrooms and spew to his heart's content. They were not compatible in any way, the princess and he. His blood tasted awful to her as she complained on the few occasions she fed off him out of anger which was fine by him. All she needed to do was not get him killed or tortured or anything else unpleasant.

Wiping his mouth off with a sheet of paper towel, he stared at his reflection in the mirror. The once proud son of a lieutenant in the Queen's army reduced to a babysitter for the princess. He had complained to his father once and was struck down. How dare he be ungrateful to be in the service of their Queen? Yes, he traveled in the Queen's circle along with the princess in the years before the school started, but now he felt like a captive in the twelve circles of hell.

"It gets better, right?" He asked his mirror image.

MAQUEL A. JACOB

FOUR: DELUSIONS OF GRANDIEUR

MAQUEL A. JACOB

CONTEST OF STRENGTH

Two and a half years of school taught Chase more than he thought possible. With every guardian safe and sound, their masters going to class as instructed, a new kind of entertainment had started to make its way into school culture. After learning about the covens some had begun taunting those in lower houses, citing superiority. He too had gotten caught up in it somehow and decided to also prove himself.

As the heir to one of the strongest covens, he basically had a target on his back every time he walked the halls. From what he had heard, Falson and Princess Adelia were in the same boat. The Dean had warned against this kind of behavior but at the same time, they all knew no one would get killed. Or so they hoped.

If another student saw a fight getting out of hand, they would intervene because if one of them got caught they were all in trouble. For that reason, a sort of makeshift housing triage was created in secret so the school nurse would never know and couldn't report to the Dean. He suspected Dean Valencia wasn't fooled but as long as there was no real damage, she turned a blind eye.

His guardian had gotten hurt a few times trying to protect both of them and he found it endearing. He was well versed in defending himself and found Baltise's lack of skill almost embarrassing.

In the cafeteria, Chase found Falson sitting at a table alone with his guardian. He decided to have a chat with the young monarch. They didn't even blink when he and his guardian sat down across from the pair. Falson mindlessly moved vegetables around on his plate.

"What has you slumming with the lower class?"

Chase snorted. "Right, because your coven is one of the higher three as is mine? You're not even close to being of lower class."

"As strong as we are, we behave like something lower."

"That's. Why would you think that?"

He was angry at that remark for some reason.

"Do you know how your guardian was selected?"

"Not really. I know they combed the lower classes of our coven for them."

"Have you ever been to the lower bowels of your castle?"

"What for? No."

Falson looked over to his guardian.

"Tell him."

Demitri hesitated for a moment and looked to Chase's guardian for; approval? He in turn glanced at Baltise who averted his gaze.

"Tell me what?" He hissed so not to alert anyone else in the cafeteria.

"Under each castle is a cavernous maze that connects to the slums on the outskirts of the towns. In those caves is where the lower-class lives."

"Preposterous! My father would never allow such a thing."

"They all allow such a thing," Falson retorted.

Demitri continued. "We were given the chance to rise out of the lower class and come into service of our masters by fighting each other. The last one standing would become guardian to the master's offspring. It was a long selection process and many of the leaders who needed a guardian for their child would attend the fights to see the outcomes."

Chase squeezed his fists tighter, drawing blood. He thought about his own guardian and relaxed a bit.

"That can't be for all the covens. My guardian is no fighter."

Demitri gave a small smile.

"He may not be a fighter but he did fight to win his new status. You think I liked fighting most of my life? I did enough to get by. But when this opportunity came up, I decided to win."

"Is that true?" He felt angry again and he was sure it probably showed in his eyes as he peered into his guardian's. "Is it?" He slammed his fist on the table. People sat up and looked over and he slumped down a bit.

"Yes." That soft response sent shivers through him as it always did.

"My father made you fight our own kind. Your people in the lower class? For what? For the slim chance to get out of the slums?"

"The top five were given that reward," Demitri interjected.

"And the ones who lost?"

"Back to their normal lives. They did get some compensation for participating."

"So, you can fight?" He asked his guardian. Baltise hung his head low and nodded.

Chase finally let it click into place. Most of the guardians didn't want to engage in conflict because that is what they had been doing all their lives. The ones who did relish in it were either feeling their new power, already too far gone to change their ways. What struck him as a no go was the selection process itself. It was like the leaders knew something else and needed guardians who could defend them.

"Wait, but from what I understand, Queen Erena's coven selected soldiers from their army."

"Not ranked soldiers. The offspring of ranked soldiers. Trained for the front lines but not full duty yet."

"How do you know so much?"

"I listen. I learn," was Demitri's reply.

Chase looked over at Princess Adelia holding court with her coven classmates while her guardian sat in a sullen state. He felt sorry for the soldier having to deal with such a master. "At some point, these altercations are going to get ugly. We all know how we got here and some of us may get overzealous for their masters."

"I won't let that happen."

Demitri stared at him in fury.

"You will be the first."

It started with a fight between two coven leaders' children and instead of resolving it themselves as usual, decided they were too important to get their own hands dirty. Protocol dictated that the guardians were to protect them at all times. So, they ordered their guardians to fight for them. Thus, a trend was born.

Chase had tried to keep away from it, not wanting his guardian to end up hurt but soon forgot about his promise earlier in the last semester.

Queen Celeste's son had purposely slammed into him in the hall.

"Humph. If it isn't the fearless leader who got all of our guardians tortured with that brilliant plan of a rebellion." He made sure his guardian stood close.

"That was your own doing. I didn't force anyone to follow my lead. You decided not to study."

"I think someone should teach you a new lesson or two." He motioned for his guardian who came at him hard.

Chase barely had time to block the blow. The guardian kept coming in fast but he held his own. Out of the corner of his eye he saw Baltise come out of the classroom with their books clung tight to his body. The books fell to the floor as he witnessed the fight. Trying to stop his own guardian from protecting him proved impossible so he ordered him to do whatever was needed in order to see Baltise's fighting skills first hand.

Changing his mind at the last moment as he dodged the talons coming at him, he ordered, "No! Stay back!"

Queen Celeste's son started to look nervous and nearly went white as his guardian found an opening and went for the killing strike. Chase braced for it, knowing it wouldn't be fatal if he backed up but there was no need. His guardian had gotten between them and the other guardian's talons sliced into his side. Chase and his guardian went tumbling down to the floor together.

As the blood pooled beneath them, Queen Celeste's son grabbed his guardian and ran down the hall. A few students who had stopped to witness the fight came to Chase's aid while others went to get help. This was the other part of the deal. When a battle occurred, no one was to interfere unless absolutely necessary.

Curing himself internally, he held onto his guardian. Another student was putting pressure on the wound to ease the blood flow. He didn't like how some of the guardians enjoyed in the fights and he had no intention of letting his do the fighting for him. Especially when the battles were brutal.

"I'm okay," his guardian whispered before falling unconscious.

It was remarkable how rampant the fighting spread over time. What was even more insane were the guardians whose masters initiated the fights, so eager to engage in them. Something was off about that but he chalked it up to the effects of the selection process.

A group of students stopped in the center of the hall on the housing complex's third floor, watching with bated breaths at Princess Adelia along with

Lariod square off with Count Marchand's son and his guardian.

"Little princess off to sneak into town to fetch a new toy?"

Rumors about her escapades were confirmed one night when Count Marchand's son caught her but didn't report it. Instead, he made sure everyone except the faculty in the school knew about it. She was treated like a pariah by some, but respected for her boldness by others.

"Hmm. I was thinking about it."

There was no use in denying she liked the attention.

"You're nothing but trash."

"Since my mother's coven is one of the oldest and strongest in our land, I would say I am worth far more than you. If anything, you should bow at MY feet."

She had learned about her coven in history class last term and loved rubbing it in the lower house students' face. He tilted his head towards her and his guardian rushed her only to be stopped and pushed back by Lariod. The other guardian tried again but her guardian was a brick wall. She laughed knowing he had the advantage as a former soldier even if he was of low rank.

"Are you done?" Lariod asked Count Marchand's son.

Angry for not being able to land a blow, the guardian extended his talons. Lariod raised an eyebrow. The guardian lunged forward and was sent flying back, blood spurting out of his mouth as he landed at the first row of spectators' feet. His charge turned away and ran to him.

"I guess he was," Adelia laughed again.

The fight over as quickly as it started, she went to her room with Lariod in tow. Flopping on her bed she kicked off her loafers.

"That was tedious. Is there no one who is a good challenge for you?"

"How about I'd rather not be fighting at all."

"You're a soldier. It's good to get some practice in. You'll get rusty if you don't use it."

"That's different."

"No it's not," she snapped. "A battle must be fought and won, regardless of the circumstances."

"You really don't understand."

Her guardian took off his shirt and went into the bathroom. She heard the water running in the shower moments later. It bothered her that he had such feelings towards the whole duel thing in the school. It was a way to kill time and get some action in. What didn't she get? Shrugging it off, she fell back on her bed and closed her eyes. A smile spread across her face. She was Princess to one of the strongest covens. That made her proud.

Baltise sat cross legged on the chair at their dorm room desk and stared at the notebooks. In female form per request, she had donned on a long shirt when they returned from the last class and started on constructing notes. Her master had gone to frolic with other students in the commons. They would be going on another break in three days and she tried to get him to stay and study for a little while.

He had backhanded her, knocking her to the floor. He attacked, feeding greedily off her then left her partially drained and hungry. Her eyes were blood red as she sat, her hands trembling. She would have to leave the room to get something to eat soon if he didn't come back before dawn.

Whenever he said, trust me, she became anxious. On one or two occasions, he had slipped and she ended up being tortured. Not as badly as the previous times, but nonetheless unpleasant. This time she knew he would not comply. Since the battles started and guardians became the entertainment, her master had changed. He indulged in it, often being the taunter and stood back watching her get beaten with a smile on his face. She didn't like fighting and dodged more than defended.

Sometimes that made him angry and he let the battle go on longer than it should. A few times, other students intervened or the other guardian was ordered to back off, the battle not being any fun.

Her talons started to extend and she fought them with sheer will. She couldn't wait any longer. Pulling on a pair of leggings, she opened the door and headed towards the cafeteria. The halls were empty until she got closer to where the housing complex, cafeteria and school intersected. A few groups were scattered here and there. As she was about to enter the cafeteria, a voice called out from behind.

"Well look at this. Chase's little guardian all alone in the dead of night."

Alarm bells went off on her head.

"And a girl too. This should be fun. Get her."

She turned in time to see Count Durante's son and his guardian standing not ten feet away and his guardian propelled himself at her. Taking a quick step sideways she managed to avoid his fists but he pivoted at high speed and got her in the ribs. It hurt more than she expected but it was not too bad. He kept coming, landing a few punches when she wasn't fast enough which she did on purpose. The Count's instructions were clear. She was not to let anyone know how strong she was.

But, now the guardian's talons were out and he was angry at not being able to put her down fast. At twice her size, he could hurt her bad if she didn't at least try to defend herself. While she pondered this, he took advantage and sliced at her with inhuman speed. She screamed as they tore into her flesh and then she was down the hall in her master's arms.

Count Durante's son and his guardian were still near the cafeteria entrance but the mob of people were yelling and pushing them in anger. Chase had red eyes and drool trickling from the side of his mouth as his fangs detracted. With her still in his grasp, he flew back through the housing complex and up the stairs to their dorm room.

There, he threw her onto the floor.

"Stupid, sow! Why were you outside this room? I told you to stay here."

His rage was palpable and it scared her. She whimpered as she tried scooting away but he followed her relentlessly.

"Hungry," she replied softly.

"Food? You nearly got us all in trouble over your greedy appetite?"

His hands went around her neck and he dragged her up into the bed. His face was contorted like that of a beast and he ripped shirt and leggings down the middle in one swipe of his talons. He held her down by the neck as he used the other hand to removed his pants and force his cock into her like a knife. She cried out in pain but he didn't care. She could feel blood trickle from between her thighs as he grunted and thrusted; A wild beast out of control. She passed out from the pain, letting the darkness take her.

Chase was in the throes of madness when he felt Baltise's body go more than slack. His vision cleared enough for him to see the wall in front of him so he looked down. There was tiny blood splatter on her breasts and abdomen. Looking further he saw it was coming from her womb, the last thrust spraying more. In horror, he stopped and climbed off her. Her veins were visible and he knew what that meant.

"No!"

He leaned over and placed a hand on the side of her cheek, trying to get a feel for blood flow. When there was none, he panicked. It all came flooding back to him. How he had nearly drained her before he left for the commons and all the blood loss from the unsanctioned battle in the hallway. Her soft reply that she was hungry and he had indeed left her that way without thinking.

Grabbing a sweatshirt and clean pants, he yanked open the door and fled back to the cafeteria. Luckily no one else was around but knew the stench of blood on him was strong. No doubt, if anyone entered the hallway there would be trouble. Reaching his destination, he grabbed two large chunks of raw meat and as much fruit as he could carry then raced back. The faculty in charge didn't have time to protest, he was in and out so fast.

He created a blockade against the door using the desk as a barricade. The meat he tore up into smaller bits and forced some of it in Baltise's mouth along with pieces of fruit. At first nothing happened and he feared the worst, if he had to give her some of his own blood that was fine but she was so far gone that it wouldn't be enough.

"Please."

I need you!

His telepathic message was loud even to himself and he was amazed at it desperation.

A slurping, gnawing sound came from her lips and hearing the portions being consumed he felt relief. He immediately prepared more, giving her a little at a time until halfway through, her eyes red as the blood in her veins opened. It slowly subsided as the food neared its depletion.

"I'm so sorry," he whispered.

Leaning over her he laid down on top of her and buried his head in her bosom. He felt her small fingers linger in his hair for a moment before flopping back down beside her. She was fast asleep. Looking up he saw the early signs of dawn and closed the shutters. He sat up and really took in all the blood. There was no way he could let her sleep in such filth.

Barely able to keep his own eyes open, he went to the bathroom and wet a handful of rags. He wiped her down and pulled the drenched sheets off the bed. As he stripped off his clothes he saw the bloody patch of pubic hair and red dots on his thighs and scrubbed them hard with one of the wet rags. Not quite satisfied with the cleanup but having no more strength to finish, he tossed the rags on the floor and laid back down next to her. He wrapped the blanket around them.

Ambrook Coven

Back in the castle for break, guardian and son went separate ways. Chase was still agitated from the incident over the weekend and felt he couldn't trust himself alone with Baltise. Instead of heading to their room, he went to find his friends and see what they were up to for the night. Strolling along the halls, he found himself walking straight in the path of the Chancellor.

Oh great. Another pop quiz.

To his amazement Chancellor Rayne stopped in front of him and genuinely smiled.

"So good to see you, young master. How has school life been treating you?"

Leery, Chase tilted his head back. "Just fine. Learning a lot."

"Good, good. And how are you treating your guardian? Nothing unsavory or dangerous I hope."

So, that's it.

"I assure you, no one suspects anything."

"Why would they. The only way they would get a hint of it is if your guardian fought someone there and I'm sure that's not the case since we don't fight our own."

"That's not how the selection process went," he sneered.

Chancellor Rayne leaned forward and his stare burned into him like coals.

"That was necessary. Outside of that, we have rules, young master." He drew away from him and smiled again. "Enjoy your stay at home."

As he walked off, Chase felt a chill go through him. Something nagged in the back of his mind. An important thing that he should know.

Cobwebs stirred in the cool air seeping between the jagged stone walls. Chancellor Rayne leaned back mesmerized by the artwork created by unseen spiders. Along the dimly lit corridor he spotted the place he had been looking for. He could tell it was the final destination by the scarcity of things in the small hole used as a home. This is where the young master's guardian used to reside.

Among the few things left behind, he gathered no clues to the enigma's bloodline. He was no closer to an answer as to what or where the gender shifting vampire came from. In the corner, he spotted old dried up bones and an inspection of them revealed how much the little thing ate. Combined with the other information he had gathered there were three possibilities.

Done with his scavenger hunt, the Chancellor made his way back to his research lab in the upper level of the castle. Old ancient books dating back to the start of the clans were kept there and he needed to delve into their delicate pages for the answer.

A soft tap on the chamber door made the Chancellor look up in annoyance. Seeing it was his master, Count Ambrook, he changed his expression to a warm one and smiled.

"Come in, my lord. Please, have a seat."

He patted the leather chair across from him as he hefted the large book he was reading onto the desk between them. Count Ambrook made himself comfortable and waited.

"I have a few theories about our greedy munchkin."

"He's not that small."

"For a vampire of our coven, he is."

Count Ambrook waved that notion away and averted his gaze.

"Anyway, I believe there are some options."

"Tell me."

"The first is that he's anemic to the point of needing more blood. But, that contradicts his overwhelming strength."

"So that's out. Next?"

"A berserker. They feed a lot and have tremendous strength. Of course, they are also prone to shifting into horrid beasts when in a frenzy."

"He is not that either. We would have seen that long ago. He wouldn't have gone unnoticed even in the slums."

"Correct."

"Which leaves?"

Chancellor laid his hand on the book and flipped to a page near the end. He smiled wide showing half extended fangs.

"Something ancient, something powerful." Count Ambrook tried to look at the page but his hand was in the way. "What have we been looking for all these centuries?"

The Count's eyes went wide.

"That's impossible." The Chancellor moved his hand so he could finally see what was on the page. "A Voshlin!"

"If I am correct, we cannot let anyone know what he is."

"My son," the Count began.

"Is going to get many killed if he continues to use his guardian like a prize fighting pet. He will not be able to contain him if pushed too far."

"Of all the stupid things our offspring could come up with, battles inside the school for sport is at the top of the list."

"We may have to prepare for the worst."

They both stared at the hand drawn image of the ancient creature and shuddered at the thought of something like that running loose in their lifetime. At the same time, they both knew it would be the tipping point in any battle they faced going forward. As long as it could be controlled.

Falson sized up his opponent in the hall and grimaced. He too liked to handle his own fights but this time he felt it was not going to be any fun for him.

"Take care of him," he ordered his guardian. When he didn't see movement from behind him, he turned to see what he was doing. Demitri stood hands down at his side staring at the other guardian.

"Are you really going to do this?" He asked the other guardian.

The response was a lunge and Demitri stopped it with one punch, pushing the other back.

"What the hell are you doing? Finish it!"

"I told you before. I don't want to fight."

His opponent laughed and said, "Pussy! You couldn't beat either of us anyway."

"If you think so."

Both master and guardian grew talons and came at him.

"So be it."

Falson backed away from the circle of mayhem and watched gleefully as his guardian beat them one after the other. When a large splatter of blood flew towards him, he clenched his fist.

"Stop!"

Talons half raised dripping blood, Demitri halted and walked backwards to him. He felt frustrated and angry with himself for forgetting that his guardian would keep going until he ordered him not too. It was an act of defiance on his part, shifting the responsibility of another student's life in his hands. The only solace was that his guardian was nowhere near as bad as some of the lower coven students.

"Come. Let's go before the trouble starts."

He saw some of the bystanders rush to the two students' aid and call for a triage person. A sudden illness came over him and he remembered his guardian telling him and Chase that this would get ugly. Now he was seeing it more clearly and realized the one thing he should never let his guardian do was fight his own kind. He felt no better than his father.

"I'm ordering you to defend me!"

Princess Adelia's shrill voice grated on his nerves and he squeezed his eyes shut at the pitch.

"Not a chance. He's half my size."

"Seems like your guardian doesn't know who to take orders from. Guess no one in your coven has any respect for you." Her opponent took a bite of his beef jerky stick and chewed like a cow. "I would never tolerate such disobedience." He nodded to his guardian and the vampire came at them.

"Guardian!" She yelled at him.

"Princess." He shrugged. "Fine then!"

Princess Adelia met the other guardian head on and landed multiple blows before he could get at her. His master, fearing for his safety decided to join in on the fray but Adelia's guardian moved between them, blocking his advance. Without turning, he called out to the Princess.

"I think that's enough."

The other guardian went sailing past him, knocking into his master and they both went down hard. He shook his head in pity and went back to the Princess' side. She actually spat blood out of her mouth and wiped it with her sleeve. It was so unladylike that he stared at her in awe.

"Let's go."

She turned away and began walking off to their next class. He reluctantly followed. This battle fiasco was going to have a turning point and he hoped he wasn't around to wit- ness how it ends. What he did know was that blood would fill the halls.

OVER THE LINE

Chase walked the halls in triumph after a successful battle, the words of the Chancellor long ago faded away and his guardian now bruised badly. One of his coven classmates followed at a safe distance. His mother had asked that he watch over her son due to the rumors she had heard but he didn't have the heart to tell her that he was the one initiating much of the battles he participated in. The guardian was having a hard time carrying their books in his beaten state but there was no one to help him.

Almost four years were up since the start of school and Chase seemed to have learned much but forgotten coven etiquette. It was like he had reverted to his old self except with more cunning and purpose. This was not how he wanted the leader of his coven to act. He hoped that when he did take over eventually, all this nonsense would be out of his system.

The two came up to their dorm room and entered. The coven classmate and his guardian stood on the other side across from it and waited. He was sure

Chase would come out soon to head to the commons. A sort of holding court over his minions type of deal went on lately. Princess Adelia and Falson had no part in it, avoiding him like the plague. As horrid a person the Princess was, she at least held herself to some ethics which he found odd. She was the first person they all thought would turn out to be what Chase is now.

From the other side of the hall came Count Durante's son and guardian. The two spies tensed up and backed further against the wall. They were known to be vicious and barely kept within boundaries of the battles. Chase's door creaked open and he stepped out as Count Durante's son and guardian came within close view. Both parties halted and then an awful smile came from Chase.

"Guardian! We have company."

Already worst for wear, his guardian came out from behind him and he too tensed in fear.

Count Durante's son sniffed and rubbed the bottom of his nose. His guardian's eyes started turning red and talons followed.

"Mr. Big shot who thinks he can lord over everyone because his father set this all up. I don't think anyone has taught you a real lesson yet."

"Oh really? I have learned a lot over the years. You'd be surprised," he taunted.

"But not to know your place."

He motioned to his guardian.

At first Chase blocked the assault but then Count Durante's son gave him the drop and he went down. The two vampires were hell bent on tag teaming him so he grabbed his guardian and shoved him into the fray.

"Defend me, damn it!"

His movements were slower than normal due to the still fresh injuries and he sustained more as Chase used him as a shield whenever the tag team got close enough for a direct hit. Blood was everywhere and that was enough for the two spies.

"Stop it. You're going too far!"

When the two didn't relent, they got into the fray but Count Durante and his guardian were not to be denied. They came at them fiercer, attacking all four of them. The looks in their eyes told the spy that they were indeed intent on killing Chase along with his guardian.

"Help us! Somebody!" The spy managed before Count Durante's son landed a punch that sent him crashing into a wall. He heard something snap and felt pain in his shoulder.

He watched helplessly at the two still trying to get through his guardian while Chase he lay on the ground in the same state, not being of any use.

A group of students came running down the hall, Falson and Demitri among them. Seeing the situation, Falson also tried to interfere.

"What are you doing? Stop!"

He was able to get his talons into Count Durante's guardian and toss him away but the son slammed into him, knocking him out of the way. His guardian caught him before he hit the ground. Then something strange happened. Baltise, losing way too much blood, changed. His eyes turned so red, they glowed and his talons grew long and sleek like black lacquer. Every visible vein turned a deep purple.

No one saw him launch at the two assailants and there was a blur of color as the three fought at high speeds. Chase's face contorted in terror and he reached out towards them. The whirlwind finally fell apart and all three bodies went flying in different directions. Baltise came at him and it seemed to take everything he had to move into position and catch him.

The Dean stood in what had been the center of the melee. She looked around at everyone present and then her gaze landed on Chase. He sat on the floor crying profusely.

"Help me! Please," he cried. His arms held his guardian close to him as he rocked uncontrollably. "Please!"

The walls had been decorated with a splash paint treatment made of blood all along the first half of the hallway. The spy lay slumped taking it all in. He chastised himself for not stopping it before it started, battle rules be damned. The nurse and her assistants flooded the scene. From his viewpoint while an assistant checked to see how bad his shoulder was, he saw the nurse place a hand over Baltise's forehead and shake her head.

"He's nearly gone. That last push was the end of his strength. A last ditch effort to defend himself. His survival instinct finally kicked in but it was far too late."

"Please," Chase whispered.

He too was far from okay. An assistant came to take him away and he went into battle mode once again.

"Don't touch him." In an attempt to stop her, he faltered from his own injuries but wasn't giving up.

"Tame him." The Dean ordered.

The assistant hit him at the base of the neck and he fell forward. She dragged him away from his guardian and handed him off to another. The Dean stepped to the downed guardian and bent over him.

"Get him to his coven's castle. They need to seal him immediately. Take Chase as well. This will be a travesty."

She took a good look at the dark veins and black talons that did not retract. The spy knew what she was thinking because he had the same thought.

What unholy thing was Chase Ambrook's guardian?

Chancellor Rayne kept in quick stride next to the enforcer carrying Baltise as they headed to the crypt. It was used for the high-class vampires and since he was a guardian in the inner circle this is where he too would be treated.

"How long?"

"About two hours."

"Is he?" The Chancellor was tempted to check for blood flow.

"Miraculously, no. But that could change at any moment."

"Then let's hurry."

In the crypt, they found an appropriate sized coffin and laid the guardian inside. The feeding tubes that ran from the coffin down into a blood tank were attached to his body and then the coffin was sealed shut and dropped into the floor. At the control panel on the wall, the enforcer turned on the valves but the Chancellor stopped his hand from going any higher.

"We need to keep it very slow."

The enforcer seemed perplexed. He removed his hand from the lever.

"But if we lower the flow, it would take much longer to revive him and it could not be enough."

"Trust me. This one would deplete our resources in no time. Keep it at this level."

He left the crypt and went to see his master. For the first time in decades, he was in his son's bed chamber watching over the young lord's recovery along with his wife. The fight was a stain on the house of covens and the fall out would be bad. The Dean felt responsible for not nipping it in the bud a year ago when it started.

Four guards had been positioned in the hall. Two at the door and two more directly across. He nodded at them and the door was opened for him. Count Ambrook sat in a chair on one side of the bed with his head in his hand covering his face. His wife sat upright on the other side, holding her son's hand and staring out the window at the waning moon.

"My lord, how is the young master?"

"Besides arrogant and stupid?" He didn't raise his head but the tone was vile.

"Enough," his wife snapped. "There is no need to cite the obvious. He's hurt more than physically."

"You enlisted spies to keep tabs on him."

"Because you decided to turn a blind eye."

"That's not what I did!"

He took his hand away from his face and stared at her angrily. The look she returned made him flinch. Even the Chancellor stepped back a bit. Her blue eyes were electric, full of malice.

"I was assured it was under control."

"That is not the point. He had gone down a path of villainy and became a tyrant."

His master balled his hands into fists and turned away from her gaze. He agreed that they should have done better but it was too late now. The son's wounds were still visible and he could only imagine how terrible a fight it was. As for Count Durante, he had yet to offer an apology for his son's unacceptable behavior.

Taking another look at the young master before leaving he saw the pain etched in his face. As awful as he treated his guardian, the Chancellor wondered how deep his feelings for him went.

Was the cruelty all a ruse?

Chase lurched forward into an upright position from his bed and tried to control his breathing. His chest felt like it was on fire, the taste of stale blood lingered in his mouth. The room was dark and empty. Crawling out of bed to stand at the window, he opened the heavy curtains to let the moon- light in. He threw the window open, sniffing the air in search for the scent of Baltise's blood. His eyes went red as he located the source and jumped down to ground level.

He found his way into the crypt and knelt on top of the sealed coffin. His head rested on the cold metal and he cried. Using what little strength he had, he forced the coffin out of the recess in the floor and undid the seal. Baltise was inside, now female and covered in dark purple veins. Her talons had still not receded. He held her to him, careful not to disturb the feeding tubes.

Sounds invaded his senses and he looked around to see the Chancellor, followed by four enforcers, enter the crypt. They stopped when spotting him and the Chancellor held up a hand to halt their advance.

"Young master."

"Get out!"

He extended his talons ready to fight but his body felt weak, heavy. The fight had taken a lot out of him but he would stand his ground.

"You need to rest."

"I need to be here."

"We are doing everything to make sure your guardian survives. Please. You must put him back." The Chancellor caught his voice as his stare landed on Baltise. "He shifted in that state?"

"Stay away from her!"

More people came into the crypt and he noted his father among them, stepping forward ahead of the Chancellor.

"My son, please."

He hissed at him, fangs protruding and a hurt look crossed his father's features.

"I won't let you hurt her."

He buried his face in her neck, letting the tears drip on her bare skin. A hiccup racked his body.

"The one who hurt her more than anyone was you. Don't put this tragedy on anyone else."

"I know," he whispered.

The Chancellor braved the distance and set a hand on his shoulder.

"You have to set her back down in the coffin."

Reluctant, he did as the Chancellor requested, knowing he was right. He resealed the coffin and let it slide back down into the floor.

"Come."

"I'm not leaving!"

His father made a gesture and he knew what it meant. There was no way he could defend himself against the enforcers in his condition and screamed in despair as they took hold of him. He struggled in vain until a sharp prick in his neck startled him and his vision began to blur. He saw the needle out of the corner of his eye before the world folded into a sea of midnight.

176

FIVE: REBIRTH

DECLARATION

Every day the young master went to the crypt to sit for hours on top of his guardian's coffin stroking the carved embossing was a sad thing to witness but at least he had no desire to do anything else. That kept the castle at ease not worrying about him doing something that would shame them yet again.

Almost two weeks had passed and no signs of Baltise awakening. The blood flowing through the tubes was slow and steady, not backing up which meant it was getting into the body. A normal vampire took a few days to recover. So much had been used for the guardian that Chancellor Rayne checked the tanks and found one of them already half empty.

Watching the young master, he felt a sense of trepidation. If what he deducted about the guardian was true, what might come out of that coffin would still be hungry and possibly destroy them all to get a meal. He had no faith in Chase being able to restrain the thing. Satisfied that the son would be preoccupied for the remainder of the night, he went to leave the castle. A car was waiting in the courtyard to take him and Count Ambrook to Count Durante's abode. The Countess and two head councilmen were going along for the ride as well.

Since an apology didn't seem to be forthcoming, they figured it was time to ask directly for an explanation. As one of the lead covens this type of insensitivity was uncommon in lieu of the coming events. Chancellor Rayne had a small battalion on standby in case an altercation arose.

Count Durante was considered a tyrant and that's where his son learned it from. Their coven was one that reluctantly joined in the schooling plan, citing no reason to try straightening out their offspring so late in the game.

He made his way into the stretch limo and settled him- self next to his master.

"Are you feeling any apprehension?"

"Not yet. But, the first sign of hostile intent and we leave."

"If they try to detain us?"

Count Ambrook turned to him in fury.

"That would be a death sentence for them."

"I agree."

He rapped the inside window and the vehicle rolled forward.

Sapienti Coven

Sweat dripped from Falson's brow landing on Demitri's bare back as he drove his cock deeper with each thrust. He had a tight hold on his hips for stability and his head fell back in ecstasy. On the verge of coming, he leaned over to bit into his guardian's shoulder and fed. This time slowly until he released his seed and heard Demitri's soft cry as he too came with him.

He didn't care anymore if someone came in and found them. This is what he wanted and his father would have to deal with it. No more denying how he felt or trolling for women to impress the coven and defy his father. Sucking the last bit of blood from the wound and sealing it as if eating ice cream, he sat back on his knees and rubbed his guardian's back, mingling their sweat. A shudder went through Demitri's body and he let out a small laugh. This was so much better.

"Get dressed."

He smacked his guardian on the side of his ass and disengaged, letting his semi soft cock slide out on its own back into his lap. Demitri turned his head to stare at him in that disinterested silent way, hair drenched and lips still swollen from his kisses earlier.

"We have a meeting with the council today." He smacked him again. "Come."

His guardian settled backwards then sat up, arching his back like a feline. He took his hand and led him into the bathroom where he turned on the shower before they both got in.

"We should dress in something business like."

"A suit?" Demitri asked.

"It's been a long time since I saw you in one and it would make a good impression on the council."

They touched foreheads and stared into each other's eyes.

"If that's what you want."

"It is. You're such a beautiful man and yet you don't know it. I want to show you off more."

His guardian sighed, the water cascading down his face and curving off his lips. He nudged his head upwards until their lips touched and he kissed him. Resting his forehead back on his, he ran his fingers down Demitri's sternum.

"What are you thinking about?"

"Him."

That was all the answer he needed. He too was thinking about Chase Ambrook's guardian. The way he changed and fought was not normal. When a vampire loses a fight, they revert to human form. He did not. The Dean made it clear not to divulge what happened to his father or anyone else.

"Do you think it matters?"

"I do."

"Then we don't tell them anything." He entwined his fingers with Demitri's. "Stay with me."

"I'm not going anywhere."

The council meeting was packed. Every high born vampire in the coven was present to hear what his father had to say. He already knew it dealt with the bad blood between some of the other covens. The incident between Count Durante's son and Chase was nothing new. It merely brought the issue to a head.

In matching three piece suits, his guardian in royal blue and him in deep purple, they made their way to the front of the room. His father gave him a lowly glance and went to his seat. Hurt by it, he went to turn back but Demitri blocked his path and shook his head. Defeated, he sat down on the opposite end of the table away from his father.

"Please be seated and let's begin," his father's lead councilman yelled out.

The attendees shuffled to their designated seats and brought their grumbling to low levels.

"As you know, we have had incidents with the other clans. This must be remedied post haste. I have spoken with our master and have devised a plan of action."

The murmurs grew loud again.

"Why don't we teach them a lesson by attacking their workforce?" One of the highborn blurted out. Voices of consensus erupted.

"And they in turn to us and so we come into a vicious cycle?" The head councilman replied.

The room hushed. No one wanted a long drawn out fight that would undoubtedly lead to casualties on all sides.

"I propose we all go out and touch base with our friends and try to convince them we need to work together. In this new era it is even more imperative that we become one nation of vampires and not a divided front."

His father frowned yet nodded in acceptance. Then he stood.

"I am going to a meeting this night with Count Durante to explain his son's recent actions. From there I will set up a conference with the lower branches to see what can done."

"Count Ambrook and Queen Erena will also be present. We are counting on all of you to do your parts in changing our relationships with one another."

"Dismissed," his father said.

The head councilman turned to him.

"Good thing you are dressed impeccably. The car is waiting downstairs. We leave at once."

As they rose, his father gave them a dirty look and went on ahead with the other councilmen in tow. He concluded it was because of his relationship with his guardian. The head councilman confirmed this.

"It seems you will not be giving him any heirs. Shame really. You could have any woman you want and it's not like you haven't done the deed with most of them. One planned pregnancy with a princess wouldn't hurt."

"He has other sons," he spat. "I have no desire to breed with any of those whores."

"Suit yourself. But don't play dumb as to how he feels about it. You are his first born and abandoning the idea of an heir for some plaything from the slums is a slap in the face."

He let his talons extend and raised it to the councilman's neck.

"He is not a plaything to me," he sneered.

"So be it. I'm not the one you should be appealing to."

With that, the councilman walked off and his guardian nudged him to follow. They had to be dignified for at least this night.

Count Durante's castle was grey and dreary, the gloomy early morning sky cast deep shadows coloring the walls charcoal black. It had the appearance of a behemoth though smaller than some of the other castles. Only about three hundred vampires were in the coven and from the rumors, they were all battle hungry and blood thirsty. Any time a human went missing over the decades they were the first to look towards and it was usually the correct answer.

A large wolf paced on the top steps of the entrance, its yellow eyes never wavering from the new arrivals. Count Ambrook stepped out of his vehicle and watched it. At some point its master would have to call it off if the coven truly wanted this meeting to occur. Queen Erena's vehicle pulled up and as she exited from the rear, she too saw the massive beast. Princess Adelia leapt out of the car and marched up to the beast, her guardian trying to catch up and bring her back.

"Oh let her do it."

From behind them, Count Sapienti stood at the door of his vehicle and waved the Princess on.

"That is my daughter you're encouraging to engage that monster."

"And from what I hear, quite fearless as it turns out."

Princess Adelia and the beast matched each other's pace then stopped. The wolf growled and let out a roar that sent spittle flying, its large teeth exposed as the lips pulled back further. The Princess didn't move. She was not impressed. When the wolf was done with his display of power, the two stared each other down at close range. Then the castle doors flew open.

"I don't appreciate your child taunting my castle guardian."

Count Durante himself stood in the entryway, dark hair straight as lines whipping around him in the cool breeze. He wore a grey suit with silver chain on the vest and a full length black velvet cloak. It was like seeing a character out of the Renaissance era with a slight modern twist. His cold eyes looked down on them in disgust.

"If you had come to fetch him sooner, she wouldn't have been obliged to toy with him."

The large wolf morphed into human form and towered over the Princess. He wasn't affected by the cold in his nakedness. Princess Adelia had a close view of his partially erect cock and she tilted her head to the left then right, approving of the sight. The werewolf kept his gaze on her as she did so. Lariod finally pulled her away, forcing her to turn her head from him.

Count Ambrook closed his eyes. The look on the princess' face was of lust and the last thing the covens needed was one of their princesses mating with the house pet of another coven. He turned to Queen Erena who struggled to hold herself back from striking her idiot child. The feeling was one he knew well.

"Count Durante. Have we mistaken the time? Are you not prepared to receive us?"

"We were just getting some last-minute preparations in order." He smiled.

Focusing on the rear of the castle, Count Ambrook caught a glimpse of a group of soldiers marching into the side entrance. He was certain it led to the halls near the throne room. A look back at his Chancellor and they nodded at each other.

"Well then," Count Durante cooed. "Please, enter."

It had been over a century since he had set foot in Count Durante's castle and noticed that it was somewhat darker. The lights were dimmer than usual and there were torches instead of lightbulbs on the walls. Condensation formed on the stone making it slick to the touch. As they reached the corridor where the throne room was located, everything changed. Hyper white bulbs lit up the area and modern decor was placed strategically in all the right places.

Inside the throne room, a bar had been set up in the far corner and there were plush sofas arranged in the center with the throne set a little higher up from the floor. It too had comfortable pillows. The group settled down onto the sofas and servants came to take their drink orders. Coven leaders came in and sat across from them with dour expressions. Count Durante went to his throne and his son sat below on the plush seat next to him. His guardian sat further behind him on a larger cushion.

The contrasts of styles within made Count Ambrook's head swim. As if the coven had no sense of what they wanted to convey. Drinks in hand, everyone took a few sips then set them down on the designated coasters.

"So, Count Durante," Count Ambrook began. "We seem to have a dilemma. Some of your coven members have targeted others and I am perplexed as to why."

"Right to the chase, hmm?"

"I think it only best," Queen Erena said.

"Some of us in the lower covens feel oppressed and against better judgement, lash out. We too would like to advance to a higher status."

"Is that your reason?" Count Sapienti snapped.

"Did I say that was my position?" Count Durante glared down at them. "I am merely making an observation based on SOME of my coven members' behavior."

"Yet, you have not tried to correct this?" Count Ambrook cocked his head.

"What are you implying, Count?" The name left off from the honorific made everyone tense.

"I too am only stating an observation. Your son and his guardian attacked mine and had all intent and purposes of murdering them on school grounds."

The son in question raised his head in anger and made eye contact with him. That murderous stare told him plenty. Fists balled up tight sitting on his lap twitched and Count Ambrook knew the boy was a split second away from assaulting him and everyone else in his party. His guardian perked up and laid a hand on a short blade lying beside him.

Count Durante let his focus move to where he was looking and frowned.

"I did not invite you here to incite a fight."

"It does not come across that way," Count Sapienti said.

He also tilted his head.

"If you so much as flinch, I will end you," Count Durante hissed down at his son.

The sideways glance up to his father would have stopped a prey dead in its tracks. Father and son glared at each other before breaking it off.

"I came for an apology whereas the others have come for an understanding."

"Apology? For what exactly? Your son became the instigator of these battles and because his guardian got hurt my son must feel sorry? I think not."

"No one is contesting that!" Falson stood up. "What we all take offense to is his blatant refusal to stop and disregard for the rules when we had to intervene. Myself and my guardian were also injured in the fight."

His father's head enforcer took hold of his wrist and motioned for him to sit back down. Wrenching from his grasp, Falson did.

"For him to go so far, means you sanctioned such behavior. Did you really think you could get away with killing the offspring of coven leaders?" Queen Erena lifted her drink and took a sip. Her stare also conveyed malice.

"I did no such thing!"

"Did you not say your coven wanted a rise in power? That would require the elimination of the top five to make yours the head."

"That's right," Count Durante's son sneered. "And thanks to my father's weakness, three of the top five leaders are here."

Count Durante was confused by this and Count Ambrook realized what was happening at that moment. The soldiers from earlier came rushing in to surround them and his son's guardian moved to strike down his master. Queen Erena was between them in a flash and sent the guardian across the room. He was quick to recover, already within striking distance again.

Count Ambrook saw his Chancellor blowing into the small reed to signal their own soldiers right before Count Durante's son came into his side view and he had to dodge the vampire's talons mere millimeters from his neck.

The throne room had turned into a battlefield. On one side was his soldiers along with Count Durante's elite personal force against his son's new army. The doors had been sealed so that no one else in the coven could come to their master's aid.

"Stop this madness!" Count Durante commanded his son.

He answered by nodding to his guardian who once again came for the Count's life.

"You have to do it," Queen Erena said to him and stepped away to let Demitri clash with the other.

In the chaos of the blood spilling, Count Durante flew into his son and grabbing the broke metal rods from a decorative room divider drove them in, impaling him to the wall. Five in all held the boy's body in place and he choked on his own blood. Count Sapienti had taken out the soldiers blocking the doors and unsealed them. Vampires flooded into the room and made a semicircle around their master. In the hall beyond, the son's loyalists were stacked in a bloody pile.

"This is not how we come to power!" Count Durante yelled at his son. "What you have done is torn the fabric of our relationship with the other covens. This is why I sent you to the school. I was reluctant at first but weighed the outcome. You have proved to me my worst fear."

"Count Durante," Queen Erena said calmly.

He whirled around on her, his eyes glowing silver.

"I will not kill my son!"

Count Ambrook watched his fellow coven leader fight back tears of hurt before turning attention back to his helpless son, now a wall ornament. He remembered fearing his own son going down a wrong path, but nothing of this magnitude. A kind of sorrow for the Count welled up in him.

"You will be sealed for the next twenty years. Only then will I consider having a conversation with you." Count Durante turned to his elite force. "Take him and his guardian. They will both endure the same fate."

As the battle died and Count Durante plopped down on a tattered sofa, his throne mangled, he placed his head in his hands.

"You knew this would happen." He addressed this to Count Ambrook.

"Not exactly. Like you, I was taking precautions in case you would try to overthrow us."

"We had no idea. You should have told us," Count Sapienti said in anger.

"Even if he had, I would have found it preposterous." Queen Erena brushed off her gown, smearing droplets of blood into streaks. "That being said, I am not so weak as to let a small army such as this take me down. As disgusting as my daughter is, she too would have cut down the enemy."

"I am," Count Durante sighed heavily, "ashamed."

"No need for that. We all knew our children had issues. Some more than others." Count Ambrook tried to reassure him.

"Accept my deep apology for your son and his guardian."

"Accepted. Now, shall we have another drink before resuming the other part of our meeting?"

"That would be ideal."

De Luce Coven

Adelia's room felt empty even though Lariod was sitting on his bed only a few yards away. He was polishing his sword, oblivious to her state of mind. Hearing her mother call her disgusting negated the praise that came after. She had resolved to not let anyone see her falter and continued on but she was losing that battle. Like a wrecking ball, her wall shattered and she burst into tears, her attempts to stop the flow in vain.

Her guardian dropped his sword and shot up from his bed in a panic. She could see his figure through a haze of tears move towards her so she clambered backwards all clumsy, not moving her hands from her face to stifle the cries that tried to escape. His arms circled her and she felt the heat from his body grow closer until she could hear his heart beating.

Neither spoke, her unable to as she stopped her inner fighting and let the flood gates open. She screamed and cried, clutching the front of his shirt with all her strength. He pulled her tighter, muffling the sounds. He was the last person she wanted to comfort her but knew he was the only one who could.

Exhaustion hit her like a freight train and her body slumped, a giant wet noodle ready to tear from its own weight. Lariod kept his hold on her even as she slipped into a tunnel void of light or anything else.

Lariod watched her turbulent sleep and wished he could find a way to alleviate her suffering. She was a pain in the ass, but he had developed an affinity for her over the short few years. That fearlessness, her superiority complex and total control over what she wanted to do with her body made him respect her. Seeing her breakdown frightened him. At the same time, he figured it would come to a head at some point. Her little charade to prove nothing could hurt her was starting to get pathetic.

In her state of oblivion, he dismantled her stylish attire. The first was taking down her twin tailed tsundere hairdo that she copied from her favorite anime. He used his fingers to bring her hair back to normal and fanned it around her. Then the corset and boots. She lay in a frilly somewhat sheer dress that went above her knees and sans underwear.

"That werewolf must have smelled all of you."

He shook his head in astonishment. It wasn't the first time she had gone out without any but he figured she would have at least done so for a formal meeting. Thinking of the brutal fighting going on in that throne room, he groaned.

Air.

He needed some air. Leaving the room, he headed out to the lower level. This time he would go out an actual door instead of taking flight after the princess through their chamber window.

Upon his return, he saw her move around in her sleep. Not the fretting from nightmares like earlier which meant she was about to awaken. He sat on the bed beside her and waited for her eyes to open. When they did, she jerked away further into the pillows.

"I am going to say this only once, Adelia." Her eyes went wide with shock at him calling her by name only. "I am your guardian and will always be on your side. Unless you do something stupid, mind you." He leaned closer to her. "Don't ever scare me like that again."

Her eyes began to well up with tears again. He slid off the bed and went back to his own.

"You're not going to stay and comfort me?" She sniffed, pulling the covers to her.

"Princess, I am not your lover or have any intention of being one."

"That's not what I meant!" Her angry face made him laugh.

"Haven't I done enough of that?"

"Wasn't even conscious," she muttered softly.

"Rest up. I have a feeling that won't be the last coven to rebel."

"Gearing up with your sword?"

"My sword is your sword," he replied nonchalantly.

She blushed. He spurted out another laugh and she frowned at him.

Ambrook Coven

Sleeping in the crypt for hours at a time was killing his back but he couldn't care less. Chase sat up and stretched before leaning over the sealed coffin that still held his guardian. Another two weeks had passed and she still had not awakened. At the Chancellor's behest, he didn't pry the coffin open to take a peek at her. Some nights he found himself in his room, gripping his erection to ease his urges. The only one he wanted was Baltise.

He had heard about the coup at Count Durante's castle and felt equally ashamed for becoming, in his eyes, something like that. Not realizing it, he had thrown all his new convictions out the window for temporary glory. In the end, he was the one who got hurt. His fingers traced the ornate carvings of the coffin and his mind fell into a hole of nothingness.

A loud bang drew him out of his reverie and he looked down at the coffin. Another bang sent the coffin rattling. He scooted back as a deep vertical crack formed. The alarm sounded to signal an awakened vampire and within moments, the Chancellor, his father and four enforcers came rushing in.

The coffin busted apart and pieces flew out like an explosion forcing them all to shield their faces. As the debris settled, the room was swallowed up in a haze of red. They looked up in awe and Chase sat stunned.

Translucent bloody wings spanning six feet across and a good foot above spread out flexing into an open position. The dark veins running through them glistened. Chestnut colored hair cascaded all around beneath his guardian, having grown three times its length. Black lacquered talons rested on either side of her, long enough to severe a head in one swipe.

He searched her blood engorged eyes for some recognition. Her mouth opened and fangs as long as his head protruded out and a shriek that drained the blood out of him was unleashed. The others in the room also went slack and the enforcers backed away in terror. When it subsided, she spoke.

"Hungry." The voice was deep, the tone mournful.

The feeding tubes detached from her body and fell onto the floor. Chancellor Rayne immediately shut off the valves to reduce the waste of blood.

"We can't feed that!" One of the enforcers cried.

He unsheathed his sword as did his companions. Count Ambrook held up a hand.

"Do not move!"

Baltise's eyes roamed the room searching for something then landed on the enforcer. He backed away in fear, not knowing what to do if the guardian actually advanced.

Chase got to his feet, fangs and talons extended.

"You will not touch her! I don't care who it is, I will kill anyone who tries to harm her. My loyalty is to her and no one else."

"You," his father stammered. "Love her."

The Chancellor pursed his lips. He had a feeling.

WAR IS COMING

Thunder shook the ground as one hundred horses galloped across the plains. Each one held at least one rider, some two. They were what was left of a faraway clan, their castle and homeland destroyed. It was a month long journey to the other side of the world where a familial clan would open their doors to them. The enemy was assumed to still be giving chase but a group had been dispatched long ago to their final destination.

The new leader of the clan rode in front, his second in command laid across behind him as he urged his horse on. His people were beyond exhaustion, the blood supply dried up days before. His blue eyes had dulled but there was a new purpose ignited in them. He hoped he would get to his cousin before the enemy, a daunting feat. Looking back to make sure no one had fallen behind, he pressed forward. They would get there before dawn, barely.

"What is going on?"

Count Durante walked briskly down the halls in a silk lounge suit barefoot. His soldiers had scrambled and there was talk of a stampede. He reached the balcony on the east wing of his castle and focused on the distant horizon. A large group of horses came into his view and readjusting his sight saw who was in front.

"Prepare the stables for incoming and open the gates!"

"My lord?"

His enforcer was about to argue with him and he gave him a stern look. As his men went to do his bidding he got a closer look at the horde of vampires coming his way. Some were obviously injured while others were barely holding on to their horses.

"What has happened, cousin?"

He went down to the lower levels to meet up with them as they came into the castle walls. At the main gate, his cousin rode up nearly mowing him down as he pulled the reins hard to stop his horse. It reared up once then settled down. The man unconscious on the back slid towards the ground but his cousin grabbed hold of him in time before he fell.

His cousin explained in a breathless voice as he dismounted.

"Enemy is near. Some came ahead two months ago. The rest in pursuit."

"Enemy?" Count Durante frowned.

Then he remembered why they had fled the homestead so many centuries ago. His eyes grew wide and he seized his cousin by the arms.

"Two months ago?"

"I think by plane or some other transportation."

"Where is your coven leader? Where is Count Xavier?"

"Dead, as is his cabinet."

"Then who is next in succession?"

He realized as he said it, that the title fell on his cousin.

"These people?" Count Durante asked.

"All that is left. Our home is destroyed, gone."

"How did?" Count Durante didn't not have time to finish. His cousin's eyes rolled back and he fell forward into his arms.

"Open the crypt," he ordered his medical advisor. "They need blood, now."

While the remains of his cousin's clan were being taken care of he motioned for his head enforcer.

"I need to send the other covens this message. How fast can the ones on the outskirts get it?"

"If we move within the hour, not long past daybreak."

"Dawn is near. Damn it!"

"Werewolves aren't as fast as we are but they can get the job done."

"Dispatch them. This is urgent."

"So, they have come to be rid of us, yet again?"

Count Durante glanced at his head enforcer who had been with him for nearly three centuries.

"It would seem so."

"Destroying an entire vampire homestead and killing the high council. Only modern technology can accomplish that feat."

"We too have modernized ourselves. Enough, get to it."

"And you, my lord?"

"Will hold an emergency meeting."

"Now?"

"Yes, Now! Go!" His General came out of nowhere and fell into step with him. "I want a unit at every wing of the castle on full alert." The man nodded and took off. He grabbed his page. "You. Wake everyone up."

Queen Erena turned to her servant and glared. It was barely after dawn and she had been rudely awakened only moments ago. The servant seemed frantic and she had the mind to put the dullard out of her misery.

"Why have you disturbed me?"

Two of her enforcers also with looks of anxiety on their faces came in behind the servant.

"My Queen, there is a werewolf from Count Durante with an urgent message."

That bode ill in her mind. There was no reason for him to send a werewolf when he could have easily sent a vampire page.

"I'm coming. Bring him to my throne room."

"We already have."

She raised an eyebrow and quickly got dressed with the assistance of her servant. Down the hall she could feel tension. Such unusual behavior would send anyone on edge. To her surprise the entire council was present along with her daughter and guardian.

"What is the meaning of this?"

"The werewolf was told to make sure all of the high council was present before delivering the message."

She walked up to her throne and sat down.

"Speak then."

"They have resurfaced and they are coming. Some are already here. The coven of Xavier has been destroyed."

"How cryptic." Her social relations advisor snorted.

Queen Erena sat for a long time mulling over the words until the answer blossomed into a burning fire. Her eyes glowed and she hissed loudly, exposing her fangs. One by one, the council understood the message.

"What does it mean? I don't understand," her daughter yelled in frustration.

"Our enemy has found us, child." The medical advisor replied.

"What enemy? Who?"

"You were not yet born. It was why we left our original homeland."

"Why?" Her daughter asked. "Why now? What are they after?"

"Our annihilation," her guardian answered.

"That is correct."

Queen Erena turned to her General.

"Prepare our troops."

"The perimeter, my Queen?" The tall female vampire inquired.

"Concentrate on the main gates on each side and check for the skies. If they are already here with re-inforcements on the way, then they may strike at any moment." She glanced down at the werewolf. "Has the message gone out to all the covens in the area?"

"Yes. You were one of the closest along the rim. The others will get there past daybreak."

"Which means they will not know since they are sleeping. Trying to wake a vampire during the day is no fun. I would imagine their servants will put the werewolf up for the day and wait until dusk." Her social relations advisor said.

"That may be too late."

"We are closer than Count Durante. Send one of our pages to Count Sapienti and have them relay it to the next coven. By then, the messenger heading for Count Ambrook will have arrived."

"Mother?"

"I will now tell you why we really built the school for you to learn our history and culture." She was silent for a long time. Then she finally continued.

"Our home world was a major hub for trade across the five solar systems. We were a family of merchants as well as all the leaders of each coven. Each house had their own clients who they in turn worked with for generations."

"Merchants?" Adelia frowned. "Not warriors?"

"There was no real reason for us to fight but our planet did have a military. And, depending on your status, you were given a squadron of your own for security."

Adelia balled her hands into fists. Confusion etched her flawless face. Her mother continued.

"There was a coup d'état and the emperor was killed. The ruler imposed sanctions against any merchant who did not give up or share their client info."

"I don't understand. Why? For what purpose?"

"To remove our status and make us slaves. Middle men to do his bidding so he could reap the financial gains."

"A coward and a thief," one of her enforcers spat.

"Exactly. Many of us were beaten down and indeed became slaves, living in slums with only the percentage of shares the royal house deemed fair. Which was barely enough for survival."

"You rebelled." Her Master at Arms stated.

"We ran."

Even some of the elite vampires hissed at such a declaration.

"After nearly a century, our parents formed an alliance, putting petty grievances aside. Taking whatever we could, we loaded up our ships and fled our planet. Of course, the emperor had his personal militia chase us down."

"So you did fight."

"I was only around 150 or so. For our species that is still young, like a child reaching the age of eighteen. Our parents saw the pursuit and determined it was a lost cause."

"But, you are all here!"

"They sealed their children in the secondary ships onboard and launched them. Each one with the same random coordinates."

She could still remember Durante's arm around her waist, his powerful grip prying her from the dock port window as she cried and screamed. Her talons carving into the metal hull while her mother stared at her and the ship pulling away until the drives kicked in. Warships descended upon them from behind. Durante's fangs sinking into her shoulder. Draining enough to knock her unconscious.

For the first time in ages, Queen Erena shed tears of sorrow, frightening not only her daughter but everyone else in the room. A heavy silence dropped down on them.

"Are we not vampires?"

Queen Erena abruptly looked up in shock. Then she tsked.

"By Earth definition, yes. We may be quite similar and may have come before them."

"Yes. All that undead business," another advisor smirked.

"Burning to cinders in sunlight!" The Master at Arms exclaimed

"And the holy water. What kind of weakness is that?" One of her enforcers scoffed.

"Most of that folklore is disjointed. Only half of it is true." The head advisor added.

Her assistant came forward, visibly distraught.

"My Queen, if what you say is true then how is it we are not more advanced than the humans?"

"Because in order to assimilate we abandoned it. This place was so primitive compared to us when we arrived that we would stand out. Glaringly so. And over time, forgotten. We kept everything archived. Recreating a lot of the knowledge into print formats."

"And the enemy? Who are they? How is it they are here?"

"They are the emperor's royal militia. Somehow, they were able to trace the coordinates."

"The first war! Her head advisor exclaimed."

"Correct. We did a good job of decimating them and they left. It has taken them this long to return with reinforcements."

"What could they be trying to accomplish by engaging in warfare on this planet?" Her second advisor asked.

"If they cannot bring us back, then better to kill us all."

"Take you back?"

"My guess is that commerce has crumbled. We had exclusive connections and without them, trade would be a struggle. Many of our clients learned to not trust the monarchy."

An evil grin spread across her daughter's face.

"We are better than vampires." She laughed. "Much more. Question?"

Adelia's head tilted far back and her irises turned red.

"What is it, daughter?"

"Is our coven also one of the merchant families of high status?"

"Of course we are!" Queen Erena snapped.

"Hmph. Good to know."

Princess Adelia pivoted and walked proudly out of the throne room.

"Was that wise to tell her? What if she spreads these revelations?"

"It's fine. We have all agreed to tell them in light of the situation."

"And the humans?"

"We tell them nothing!" Queen Erena stood up and glared down at them. "What they don't know makes us stronger."

As she sat back down, the tension in the room lessened.

One dilemma off the table.

Sapienti Coven

Sunlight blazed the sky but its brilliance could not penetrate the heavy shutters and drapes of Count Sapienti's castle. Even so, the vampires inside knew it was morning and were already in bed. When the messenger from Queen Erena came banging the giant knocker, the guards were ready to murder him on the spot. The look of urgency on his face made them think twice. Why else would a page from another coven show up unless it was dire?

Count Sapienti was not happy and neither were his council as they assembled per the messenger's request. His son and guardian looked about as awful as the rest. The messenger stood in the center of the throne room nervous.

"Let's have it," Count Sapienti demanded.

The messenger relayed the same cryptic message but he got it almost immediately. He stood up from his throne and bore his blood red stare into the messenger.

"Are you certain?"

"Queen Erena and Count Durante have mobilized their armies. The enemy was in pursuit. They should arrive within days." The page's voice shook with fear.

"The enemy? As in the one we learned about in our private history classes?" His son sat up in shock as he asked it.

Count Sapienti scanned the room at his councilmen and women.

"This is no drill. I want every able bodied soldier ready for the front lines. The castle takes priority but the slums must be protected as well."

"Understood, my lord," his General answered. Taking his leave he went to his duties.

"We're not ready," his son whispered. "We're not prepared for such an assault in so short a period of time."

"There is no other option. This is what we were preparing you for. We knew they would show up eventually. But not now. I figured in a decade or two."

"Wait." His son looked up at him. "The school was for this?"

"There was no way any of you spoiled, inept children were going to be able to combat this crisis uneducated."

His son hung his head in acceptance. He knew he was right. Their offspring's' behavior was a signal of their doom if the enemy had shown up years ago.

"Now what?" He asked.

"We fight." His guardian had a look of conviction.

The one thing Count Sapienti could not deny was that his son's guardian was someone who could be counted on. He was ready to engage.

Ambrook Coven

Unlike the other covens in the land, Count Ambrook had to do business in the light of day on occasion. Humans operated on banker's hours, not wishing to chance a night encounter with vampires regardless how much money they had. The werewolf that came to the castle was a shock but he granted him an audience.

"I must insist that all of your council including your son be present. It is Count Durante's request." The messenger bowed politely afterwards.

He motioned for his enforcers to round up the rest. It would take a little longer since they were not prone to be awake as he. When they came into the throne room, his son maddened from lack of sleep, the message was told. At first, Count Ambrook didn't think he had heard it correctly and asked that it be repeated.

"They have resurfaced. They are." He waved the messenger off from continuing.

An invisible giant bomb imploded within his gut and he gripped the edges of his throne. He turned his gaze on his Chancellor who in turn looked to the General.

"We are not ready yet."

"I don't think that matters at this junction." Count Ambrook seethed.

His son became suddenly alert. A clarity brightened his complexion.

"The nemesis is afoot."

"What?"

"It's from an old novel we had to read in school. Our enemy has come knowing we are not prepared."

"Why do you say that?"

"Because they were already here watching. Not two months ago. Years, maybe decades ago."

"Son, how could you know something like that?"

"Because their timing is impeccable."

Count Ambrook looked at his son in a new light. He knew his son was not an idiot, only acted like one. To have such keen insight meant he would be a greater asset to the coven than he thought. He had to admit, the boy was correct. War was coming.

To accommodate so many coven leaders and their entourage, Count Ambrook had an entire hall emptied and requested each clan to contribute seats as well as food. Even then, he wasn't sure they would all fit comfortably but that was beside the point. This was not a social meeting. It bordered on being a war council. Servants flurried about trying to make it look appealing while more people filed in.

The food was placed in one section against the far wall to maximize space in the center. Barrels of spirits were stacked beside it. Seeing the mass quantity, he still didn't think it was enough.

As everyone got situated and the noise levels faded, he went to his seat in the front of the crowd and clapped his hands. All eyes turned to face him. It was past nine at night but most of them hadn't gotten much sleep in the few past days. Enemy sightings had been confirmed but they had not advanced for an attack. Having this meeting was risky given the circumstances.

"My fellow clansmen, I know we are weary but a plan of action must be devised quickly. The floor is open to suggestion."

"We will not run again!" Queen Celeste yelled out.

"That is a given," Count Sapienti snapped. "The question was how do were defend our territory." They stood to face each other.

"Sit down!" Count Ambrook commanded. "Fighting amongst ourselves is not an option." He looked for Count Durante's cousin in the crowd and finding him spoke. "How was the land destroyed? And how many invaded?"

"Bombs. Not the usual kind. Filled with acid." Gasps echoed the hall. "Disintegrated everything, even the stone walls. While we tried to save many, they attacked from the air. Two hundred, maybe less."

"How did you manage to get away with as many?"

Durante's cousin balled his hands into tight fists and bloody tears leaked from the corners of his eyes.

"I took who I could and we fled, leaving the rest still fighting behind."

Cold silence filled the hall. No one berated him for his actions. They all would have done the same. If any survived, that would be a small triumph but they all knew that was not the case. The enemy would have made sure none lived to tell the tale.

"So how do we combat a weapon such as that?" Queen Erena asked.

Always remaining neutral and never one to delve too much into coven politics, Count Marchand stood, shocking everyone. Count Ambrook sat back in his seat, intrigued by it.

"We have an underground hold on the highest technology. From my intelligence gathering, it seems the world believes us to be stuck in medieval times with a few twenty first century amenities thrown in. If that is what they think then our enemy feels the same."

He stepped up towards the front of the room to stand beside Count Ambrook.

"Look at us. We still live in old castles but ride in the latest transportation. We mingle with humans but as far as anyone can tell, we don't hunt them for a food source. We eat regular food. The enemy sees this and envisions an advantage."

"What you're saying is, we need to combat them with an even more advance weapon than what they have?" Count Ambrook inquired.

"Not necessarily. Do you remember what drove them out? Frightened them to death so many centuries ago before the attack that drove us away?"

Chancellor Rayne cleared his throat and interjected.

"Katalings and Volshins. A rare breed of vampires who died out decades before."

"From starvation. They required more nourishment than our kind could provide. We were not knowledgeable. Now we have the resources to cater to them."

"They are extinct!" Count Sapienti cried out.

"There may still be some lurking. We must find them and lure them to us."

Chancellor Rayne gave Count Ambrook a side glance. That made sense. There was no way a baby Volshin would appear without a small group of them not surviving somewhere. For now, they would keep quiet about his son's guardian but he was stunned at the coven leader's assessment of the two species survival.

"That's are great plan?" The lower seventh coven leader snorted.

"Just one of them. Do you have anything to contribute?"

"Yes! We blow them out of the skies before they can attack."

Count Durante's cousin shook his head.

"WE tried that. Their sky vessels are loaded with the acid. The stuff rained down on us as we tried to get survivors out of the rubble."

"Such gruesome aesthetics," Queen Celeste shuddered. The lower seventh clan leader sat back in his seat looking twice as pale.

"I will send an investigation team to the site and get samples of the compound. There should be some residual specimens left behind."

"How long will that take?"

"By plane? A couple of days."

"And then? You need to analyze and neutralize it, correct?"

"I have the finest scientists in my coven. Who do you take us for?"

"And what if they attack before then?"

"Oh, they won't. They're watching, waiting. This is a city with over a million humans. They don't dare make a move until their logistics are in place."

"That man frightens me," Count Durante whispered to Queen Celeste.

"I agree. But he seems to be our best hope," she whispered back.

Count Ambrook threw the crypt doors open ahead of his son and walked down the landing to stand as far away from his son's guardian as possible. The creature was sitting up in her usual posture, wings expanded. Her bloody eyes moving around scanning the room again. His son got close to caress her cheek. The eyes closed and her head tilted into his hand.

"Hungry," the thing said softly.

Count Ambrook tensed. The feeding tubes had been reconnected and food was brought in addition to lessen the burden on the tanks. To feed her anymore would bring suspicion down on them and he had no intention of letting anyone know they had an actual Volshin in their possession.

"We must go hunting for her," his Chancellor advised.

"What?"

"Somewhere along the outer perimeter of the city. The farm lands. We could easily bring back a few livestock undetected. At least for a while."

"With the enemy hovering above observing?"

"That is what the underground caves are for."

His son looked over at him.

"That is the best way. We can't starve her, father."

Count Ambrook turned around and left the crypt, the Chancellor following with two enforcers. When they reached his office, he waved the enforcers away and beckoned the Chancellor to have a seat.

"How much were they taught in the school?"

"The bare minimum when it came to before the attack and not much on the enemy."

"Typography?"

"Only the main avenues. Nothing about the tunnels or underground connections between coven castles."

"See to it."

"We're sending them back to school?"

"We're all going back. In stages. No need to alert the enemy. I'm sure they know about our offspring going there. As long as we go like normal."

"I guess I too could use some brushing up."

Count Ambrook sighed, leaning back in his chair. *Back to school.*

On the way back to their vehicle, Queen Erena's entourage glanced up in unison to the sky and saw the dark speckles in the distance. They had not moved an inch in four days. She had received Count Ambrook's instruction from a page as she was leaving the throne room. Intrigued, she decided to take a visit to the school in the coming week and do some digging herself. The school served a dual purpose by also housing all their old records. Out of the corner of her vision she saw her daughter still frowning at the thought of going back to school.

"My Queen," her head enforcer called. She stopped and turned to her. "Shall we postpone the dinner for Count Durante and his guests?"

She had forgotten about the invitation extended to them two days ago. When the enemy had not moved by the next day, she wanted to pick the cousin's brain on the matter. A few feet away from her vehicle was

Count Durante's so she nodded to her enforcer then at them. Her enforcer hurried over to Count Durante and made a hasty exchange of words. He looked over at her and also nodded.

"Come," she commanded her people. "Let's get home."

Soldiers lined the front steps of Queen Erena's castle as both party's vehicles came to a stop and the drivers opened the doors for their charges to exit. Night was in its finest hour of midnight. Princess Adelia got out of the car at the same time as another from Count Durante's group and she turned to see who. It was the werewolf guardian; a tall mountain of ripped muscles and long dark hair.

He caught her stare and she licked her lips in lustful pleasure. He snorted and went to his master's side.

"Really, Princess? You think he hasn't had better?" Lariod laughed.

"How dare you!"

She whirled on him to strike but he dodged it. Frustrated, she made her way into the castle, her eyes a constant on the werewolf, remembering his naked form in front of his castle's doors. Fighting side by side with him wouldn't be so bad either, she thought to herself. For now, she had to do more research on the enemy and her own clan. It bothered her that she had little knowledge of either and no one to blame but herself.

At the hallway of her room, she stopped at the door.

"Am I not worthy of being a part of the council?"

"I think once you prove your worth it will be a non- issue," her guardian replied.

"Am I not pretty? The men, they say so but the way they look at me. Like that werewolf did."

"It has nothing to do with your beauty."

He reached around her and opened the door.

"Then what? Why have I not found a mate in all this time?"

He pushed her in and went to his bed.

"Did you really want one?"

"Of course I do! How could you ask that?"

"So you're going after a werewolf who is not only twice your size but has no interest?"

"I'll get his attention."

She made a vow to that and as if reading her mind, her guardian let out another laugh.

"You vow on it, right? Good luck with that."

Princess Adelia cocked her head at him and wrinkled her nose. The trick was that the werewolf was one of Count Durante's personal guards. Would he release his pride and joy to be with her? Erasing self-doubt, she went to her closet and flung it open.

"What do you think? Pristine and formal or a little bit naughty?"

"Oh, Adelia," her guardian sighed. "When are you not naughty?"

"Pristine and formal it is."

She found a lemon-yellow gown that went to the floor and had a plunging neck line. The waist had a wide band to accentuate her figure. Pulling the twin ponytails down, she shook her hair out. The corset came off first, then the frilly dress and finally her Goth Lolli boots that had what seemed like a gazillion laces as she undid them.

While bent over butt naked, she moved her head to the side so she could see him. He was laid out on his bed, one arm across his chest with eyes closed.

"You have to get dressed too. I will not have you accompany me in those drab clothes."

He turned to her and winced, quickly averting his eyes. She got the boots off and walked right up to him. Reluctantly, he faced her.

"I want you to wear your army uniform. Armor as well."

"Fine. Just put some clothes on. You know I am not a fan of your," he made a circle with his fingers at her.

"Humph!"

She went to her bed and had her hand on the dress.

"Please, for the love of all that is holy, put on some underwear at least."

"What for?"

"Because pristine and formal means dignified and wearing undergarments."

She thought about it for a moment and concluded he may be right.

"Then find me some so we can go."

Her guardian sat up and looked at.

"Princess."

"What?"

"Never mind."

He walked to her dresser and opened the drawers. She smiled mischievously as he grimaced at the choices.

Serves him right.

The seating arrangement was of no concern to her as she went immediately to the end of the table where the werewolf sat next to his master's page. She was supposed to be at the other end with her council but knew her mother had no use for her being there. The werewolf turned and stared at her, their eyes locked and neither cut away.

Metal tapping on glass forced them to slowly disengage and look towards the front end of the table where her mother's head councilman stood holding said wine glass and silver fork. He set down the fork and raised his glass higher, the red liquid sloshing around.

"To our honored guests. May we combine forces and live to have a victory feast."

"How morbid," Princess Adelia muttered as she too raised her glass then took a sip.

Her werewolf tossed the wine back like a shot and set his glass down. He continued to sit in silence throughout the whole dinner, occasionally glancing at first her face then her cleavage. She smiled ruefully.

After dinner, the party was led into the sitting room to discuss strategy. She pretended to pay attention until she heard the werewolf's name mentioned. Tesul. Her gaze focused on him where he sat across from her on the opposite side of the room. He didn't look up once. A side glance to her guardian showed him amused by her vigilance.

"Your journey is long to return home. May I suggest you stay and rest? Leave tomorrow evening."

Her mother's suggestion made her perk up and the werewolf actually met her stare. As everyone got up and left her guardian grabbed her by the arm.

"Whatever you're thinking of doing, I would advise against it."

"I have no idea what you're talking about," she
hissed.

"Princess."

"Go get me something to snack on from the
kitchen."

She walked briskly to her bed chamber, aware
that the werewolf was not far behind. At her door,
she opened it and was about to close it when a large
hand stopped it. The werewolf entered and shut it
behind him. Feigning outrage, she spun on him.

"You can't just," she sputtered.

His body was so close she could feel the heat coming
off him. He smelled of wet earth after a rainfall and it
sent her senses swimming in an ocean of lust. With one
motion, he had her dress falling to the floor and himself
stripped naked while she stood immobile, mesmerized
by his eyes that never left her own.

This was a first for her. No man, vampire, human
or otherwise had ever made her react this way. Her
body refused to listen to her commands. His hands
roamed her body making her shudder and her head
fell back, eyes fluttering closed.

No! You don't submit to men. They submit to you!

Her mind screamed it but still she had no desire
to move, let alone obey.

The werewolf placed his hands under her arms
and lifted her with ease as if she were a paper doll.

He set her on the bed, pulling the stringy material that passed for underwear off and tossing it on the floor. The way he crawled atop her like the animal he was finally did her in and she felt wetness ooze out of her. With eager anticipation, her legs parted without her consent and he obliged by using his thighs to push hers around his hips.

She felt her eyes go wide as his overly large member made its way into her, stretching her labia beyond its limits and she grabbed hold of the sheets beneath her. The pain was like nothing she had ever felt, her voice unable to scream from the shock of it yet she didn't want him to stop. Her body arched up, tense as a metal spring wound too tight and ready to snap.

He leaned forward, pushing himself deeper inside and locked eyes with her once again. Never wavering with each slow and brutal thrust as her vocal chords finally decided to work. She cried out, almost a shriek to her own ears. Music to his. He closed his eyes for a moment listening then came back to staring into hers.

She was crying. The tears wouldn't stop no matter how much she willed them to. Faster. His pace increased and it was almost too much to bear. Pain, ecstasy, defeat, remorse. All of it struck her in one blow. Fangs protruded while talons punctured the mattress below through the sheets. Her eyes turned red as she felt something she had not experience but knew what it was.

With a vibrating growl from the werewolf and a last scream of release from the Princess, they came together. Still arched back dispensing his seed, the werewolf howled to the setting moon. Her vision glazed over as she struggled to stay awake, a curtain of death covering her. She felt like she was dying even though she knew it was a sleep far deeper than she could imagine.

The castle shook, wall hangings flew off walls and furniture slid across the room. Groggy but now awake, Princess Adelia sat up and surveyed her surroundings. She felt a sudden chill and saw that her window was open, her guardian crouched on the sill.

An intensity on his face let her know that something bad was happening. Tossing off the covers she went to slide off the bed and found her body was unable to cooperate. Limbs like jelly came with a sharp pain in her abdomen. She gasped, distracting her guardian briefly.

"They moved."

Her mouth gaped.

"When?"

"A little over an hour ago."

"But I didn't feel the castle shake until now."

"Because they just attacked us from the sky."

By sheer force of will, she managed to get up and make it to the window. As she looked out, her heart thumped hard with rage.

Bodies lay strewn on the pasture beyond and the ones not yet dead screamed in agony as they disintegrated into the ground. A large chunk of the castle had been blown open and the enemy was making its way in an attempt to infiltrate. Soldiers were yelling to get back in the castle.

At first she thought they were abandoning the fight in cowardice until she saw Count Marchand's people erecting large poles on either end of the property. A touch of a sensor on their edge and a strange shimmer enveloped the castle. She watched through the haziness as the enemy got within a quarter mile and were burned from the shimmering field. The ones in the front lines sizzled and cracked as they made impact.

"Are we going out?"

She clenched her fists, wanting to join the fray and eliminate the threat with her own brand of vengeance.

"Can you?" Her guardian didn't look at her but she knew what he implied.

"Watch me."

She turned away and went to get dressed. It took her a little longer to get her corset and boots on but when she was ready, she climbed onto the sill alongside him.

"Let's go."

They jumped down to ground level and fell in line with the other soldiers below. An agent of Count Marchand motioned them to the far edge of the shield and used a strange device to carve out a doorway. He stepped aside and they needed no instruction. With her in front, she led the soldiers out onto the battlefield.

The first few enemies she engaged smelled foul, like raw sewage and she realized it was their burnt flesh from slamming into the shield. Forcing herself not to vomit from the stench, she tested the next one's reflexes by swiping her talons as close to his neck as possible. He was faster than she thought, not only leaning back to avoid it but somehow maneuvered down and around, striking her in the back.

It was not a subtle blow. She tasted blood and coughed up a good amount. He came again, not willing to give her a chance to recover but she already had. Angry, she went at him, relentlessly. Her talons met his body tenfold as she executed leaps in the air between hits. The last leap she used to come down and side wind kicked him in the neck. His head came off in a ragged fashion, her swing not entirely clean. The body fell to the ground spewing black blood from the gaping wound.

Off in the distance, she found her guardian finishing off two at a time by slicing them in half in one motion. She approved and went on to take down more. Past the carnage, she saw how many had come running for the castle and hissed loudly. Hundreds swarmed the area. Up above, their air ships moved out of position. They were leaving their men to their fate.

So be it.

She as not going to let any of them live for coming to her castle. A fight is what they will get. A moment of weakness in her bones nearly halted her movements but she pushed through it and headed back into battle. She could heal faster with blood but not knowing what the enemy's would do to her, she passed on the idea. It dawned on her soon enough that this was a test and the enemy now knew they had a way to be protected from their airstrikes.

What next?

Ambrook Coven

Count Ambrook stood in horror at the scene laid before him. All around the castle there was mayhem and carnage, most of it his own kind. Count Marchand's minions had finally erected the shield but not before massive damage to the west wing. He watched the dark swarm of the enemy come across the grounds in a wave clashing with his army. There were too many.

His Chancellor busted through the chamber door and came to his side.

"I have a way to rid ourselves of them but you need to answer me right now."

"What are you planning?" He couldn't pull his eyes from the window.

"We use her."

This got his attention. He turned on him.

"Are you insane?"

"This is not the time to be secretive. We need to get rid of them. Look at our territory!"

Count Ambrook adjusted his vision to span wide and saw pillars of smoke in two other directions. He was sure if on the other side of the castle that he would see the others in the same state. High above, the enemy air ships were backing away. An indication they were toying with them.

"Fine."

Both men wrenched themselves from the scene below and headed for the crypt. The two guards at the entrance bowed slightly and opened the doors.

Baltise was awake, her eyes nearly glowing. The Chancellor shut off the valves and the feeding tubes disconnected from her. Chase was sitting next to her.

"Would you like to hunt?" Her gaze wavered.

"Hunt." Her voice was low. "Prey," she said slowly. "Hungry."

"You can eat all you want. As long as it's the enemy."

He nodded to the Chancellor who pushed the two buttons that opened the sliding stone encasing the crypt. Sharp wind blew into the room and the battle-field came in view. Chase stood, turning to see and tensed up like a board.

"You can't! There's too many!"

"Oh, I think not," the Chancellor said.

The guardian's wings flapped and she rose from her sitting position. Her body made a slow turn until she was facing the outside. She got a little higher, then the wings snapped back and she catapulted out of the crypt. A pathway of torn bodies appeared and in her clutches was an enemy she had in her mouth, draining every ounce of him. From their vantage point he could see the body literally wrinkle and decay before she dropped to grab another.

"My God," he whispered. In a panic, he gestured to his Chancellor. "Tell everyone to retreat. Let her finish it."

"Father!"

"Shut up!" To the enforcer nearby, he said, "Make sure the shield is intact once everyone is inside."

"You're going to leave her out there?"

His son grew talons and was about to come at him but in one swift move, he had him down on the floor in a death grip.

"Do you want to die? Because I guarantee if she doesn't stay out there to clean the area, the enemy will come and do exactly that. Now calm yourself and watch."

Seeing the enemy torn apart, the life sucked out of them in such speed, made his stomach lurch and he fought back vomit. It was a massacre unlike anything he had ever witnessed. One being taking down hundreds in under an hour. When she was done, her wings carried her back to the crypt where the Chancellor immediately pushed the button the seal the room.

The guardian came to settle next to the open coffin and to their surprise, morphed into human form. Her small naked body was now creamy with streaks of black blood, the wings retracted into her back.

"Did you get enough to eat, my dear?" The Chancellor asked her.

She simply nodded and leaned on Chase who had been there to catch her.

"Sleepy."

Her eyes closed and he held her tight, caressing her head.

"Well, we can't deny this now, can we?"

"I guess the enemy won't be the only ones who know we have a Volshin."

Sapienti Coven

From across the plains, Count Sapienti saw something strange near Count Ambrook's castle and snapped his fingers at his page for binoculars. His sight was far reaching but not enough to see onto the grounds of another castle. He reared back in horror as he watched the thing with red wings and flying hair cut through the enemy lines, literally. The way it drained its victims and tossed them away like garbage made him almost feel pity for the enemy.

"Volshin."

"What?" His Head Enforcer came up beside him and also motioned for the binoculars. Count Sapienti handed them to him and watched the stricken look form on his face. "They had one in their midst this whole time?"

"That would seem to be the case."

"Why? Why would they hide something like that when we need it?"

"I think they had no idea until recently. Besides, would you want to unleash something like that without first knowing it won't kill anything and everything?"

"Where did it come from?"

"Did you not see?" Count Sapienti smiled. "Look again and tell me what, or who, you see."

The man strained for a bit scanning the thing then a loud gasp escaped his lips.

"The son's guardian!"

"How convenient is that?"

The two men stood at the window and watched until the end. Count Sapienti decided more than one of those things was not ideal. He didn't want one in his coven's midst.

THE RISE OF A COVEN

With the enemy backing off after their Volshin displayed her prowess, the covens had time to put together a summit and Count Ambrook's castle was the designated site. Once again, an army of vehicles crammed at the gates letting out battle weary vampires anxious to hear some good strategy.

"Can you believe it?" Count Grieger exclaimed. "Count Ambrook's coven was already one of the three strongest and now it has risen to the top, ruling over us all."

Queen Celeste came up behind him.

"That they had a Volshin. Inexcusable."

"They probably have a Kataling as well."

Ahead of them, Queen Erena tilted her head back.

"I don't think so."

Count Ambrook stopped listening in on his guests' conversations as they entered his home. True, his coven had now become the governing body for the others but he did not see it that way. With power comes too much responsibility. As for the Volshin, his Chancellor was already scouring the last known location of her origin to see how she came into the coven. His son asked her many questions when she awakened days later from her deep slumber, having gorged herself with the enemy. Her memory was hazy at best.

The banquet hall was filled to capacity and this time his staff was prepared. His throne was polished and new cushions had been set on it along with his wife's. They would be on the platform looking down on everyone. From that height he could see how much of a toll the short lived test battle had taken on them. The enemy was cunning. If an all-out war started now, they would lose.

Count Marchand's clan settled in an area off to the side farthest away from the front. He had a Bluetooth in his ear that his assistant gave him updates with. They were all thankful that he embraced new technology on a higher scale than any of them.

He noticed Queen Erena and her group looked more tired than the others. It was rumored that everyone in the coven ended up on the battlefield, the Princess included. Having his own offspring to fight was a last resort in his book unless the demise of him and his entire cabinet was imminent. The Queen was lucky that Count Durante and his clan were at her castle.

"Ladies, and gentlemen," his Chancellor yelled out. "Please, let us begin."

"We are all aware that this was a test from the enemy and they are ramping up for a full assault. That said, I had no choice but to unleash our Volshin."

His son sat below next his guardian and many of the clansmen gave them attention with wide eyed stares. Baltise looked uncomfortable from the scrutiny. Back in male form, he was still quite docile looking.

"How many do you have then?" Count Grieger spat out vehemently.

"If I had more, you would have known about that." He returned the nastiness.

"And we're supposed to believe you?"

"Enough!" Queen Erena sat straighter. "I don't question his decision at all. If he had told us long before the enemy showed up that he had a Volshin, we would have tried to monopolize or kill it." She scanned the room and confirmed this by the looks of resentment. Count Ambrook nodded. "Now that is out of the way, I do have a confession."

The room got quiet and Count Ambrook had a sinking feeling about what she was going to say.

"I found a Kataling some twenty years ago in the tunnels." Slack jawed, Count Ambrook leaned forward as she continued. "It seemed lost so I brought it into the coven. The amount of feeding required to care for him, you know all too well, Count Ambrook."

"So, where is he?" Count Ambrook asked.

"At my castle, of course." She pursed her lips. "Exposing him to such heathens as the lower clans would have been detrimental to our cause."

"Have I seen him?" Count Ambrook stared down at her and she smiled, not answering.

"Then that strategy is in play. Does that mean each coven needs to find its own Volshin or Kataling?" Count Quinn inquired.

"That would be," Count Ambrook didn't finish his sentence.

By the way some of the clansmen's faces scrunched up he knew they understood his hesitance at suggesting it.

"Well, then our new fearless leader, what is your great plan?"

He smiled. "I believe we should let our offspring prove their worth and devise one that benefits all our covens."

Shouts of outrage careened against the walls, vibrating the tables. His wife looked at him in pity. This was all going downhill fast. As it died down he cleared his throat.

"Was the plan not to educate our children so they could take over this task when the enemy again appears?"

"But that was contingent on the enemy showing up in ten, twenty years. They are incapable of saving us," Count Grieger yelled.

His son stood up, visibly offended. So did Princess Adelia and Falson. All the offspring who had endured four years of the school were on their feet, insulted.

"You have no faith in us?" His son cried out. "Then why did you send us there in the first place. You say in ten or twenty years you can trust us. Why not now?"

The elders turned away, some in embarrassment, the others out of indifference.

"We shall prove you wrong," Falson added.

All of them walked out of the hall leaving huge gaps in the seating arrangements. Their parents watched in shocked indignation.

"Such insolence!"

"How dare they!"

"Childish and uncalled for!"

So many insults were thrown into the air for their own children that Count Ambrook let them finish before speaking.

"Are they not right?" Silence fell. "Would you have let them handle it in such a short time span? I think not. I too was leery until my son showed me he was capable of deduction in regards to our enemy."

"My daughter showed great resolve on the battle-field. I knew she could handle herself against humans and other vampires but I had never seen her like this. She is a force to be reckoned with and has regained my respect."

"As the leader of the covens, I decree that our children shall lead the way. Those of you with battle experience should guide them instead of undermining them."

He stood up, the agenda complete as far as he was concerned.

"One other matter, Count Ambrook."

He looked to see who had spoken and Count Durante stood up.

"What other matter?"

"My cousin is now the leader of his coven. How does he go about becoming part of our territory? He has no home yet."

"Until this war is over, he shall remain as a part of your coven. After that, we will check the zoning and see where he may want to reside."

He saw the disappointment on the faces of the cousin's coven and felt for them but this was not the time. Stepping down from his throne, he helped his wife down and they went to the empty seats up front.

"Bring the food and wine. I think we could all use a spirit or two right now."

"Yes," Count Grieger snorted. "After our nerves have been shot with your decree."

"Oh, shut up," Queen Celeste snapped. "Your son probably has more scruples than you could ever have in two lifetimes."

Count Grieger's face turned bright pink, his fangs protruding.

"She's right. Now have a drink."

Count Sapienti handed the incensed man a snifter of Brandy. Without a word, he downed it and held it out for a refill.

"Heaven help us all."

"Or the devil," Count Ambrook piped in.

Chase pushed open the unused study door and proceeded to the table in its center, shoving everything off it. Dust flew into the air, swirling like a tornado before settling. The rest of the coven leaders' offspring behind him coughed as they entered, some waving the dust from their eyes and brushing it out of their hair.

He threw himself into an old chair by the window and put his feet up on the stool. Baltise situated himself on the floor next to him and leaned against the decaying bookshelf. Count Marchand's twins, Olivier and Olette, perused the shelves while the others found seats around the room. They still wore old world styled clothing from their home country of France circa 1902 but with modern accessories. Without any light, Olivier's Tag Hauer watch gleamed as he reached for a book. His sister had one hand feeling along the spines of books while the other moved along the surface of her smart phone.

"Chase Ambrook," Olette spoke. "Are you also going to be our leader on this task?"

Her French accent was soothing and oozed sensuality. He watched Falson fidget knowing he had bedded the young upcoming Countess a decade ago.

"If that is the consensus, I will do it. But," he sat up and surveyed everyone in the room.

Olivier interrupted his thought. "We have to get the elders on board. You may have some insight but none of us have the battle knowledge."

"Our parents went through a war that raged for nearly fifty years."

"Your coven has connections in the French scientific world which has advanced farther than the Germans." Count Grieger's son added.

"Surely you jest!" Queen Celeste's son balked.

If he remembered correctly, his clan was of German origin. Chase decided to nip the issue in the bud before the insult turned into a confrontation.

"We are not here to squabble with each other. That is one of the reasons they don't trust us."

The French twins both cocked their eyebrows at him in unison. Count Grieger's son sat back in his seat miffed. Having them on board was going to be essential because most of the leaders' children were not very apt in fighting. He was adequate at best. In this new era, they had no need for such skills, focusing on socializing and selfish endeavors.

Counts Sapienti, Durante and Queens Erena and Celeste had armies that still did campaign drills so their covens were familiar with combat. Count Marchand and Count Grieger were well versed in the newest technologies. Not enough by his calculations.

"I propose we move into the school again." Looks of defiance crept on their faces. He sighed. "That way we are not interrupted and have the instructors on hand to guide us."

"From what I overheard" Falson said, "our parents were on board to brush up on their own history as well."

"Let's hope they hold to that."

"So now what?" One of Durante's coven sons asked.

"We create a cabinet of our own. Shall we do a vote?"

Another of Coven Marchand's children pulled a paper tablet from his satchel and sat down at the table. He took out a pen and began drawing a grid with each coven, along with their strengths. When he was done he looked up and waited.

Chase cleared his throat.

"Who wants to do what?"

Everyone made a slow lean forward to take a look at the grid, grimaces all around.

De Luce Coven

Queen Erena straightened her suit jacket and sat upright, eyeing the governor as he took a sip of his drink. He was relaxed, far back in the chair with legs crossed and one hand dangling over the arm rest. His lips smacked and he rolled the glass between his fingers.

"Should our government be worried about these airships floating on the outskirts of this territory?" His sight never left the glass.

"I don't have the answer to that."

"Why are they here? Reports say they chased a group of your kind."

"They are our enemy, yes."

His focus left the glass and zeroed in on her.

"That is unacceptable."

"We are handling it."

"First, your diabolical daughter kidnaps my son," he began.

"That is not what," Queen Erena relied, but was cut off.

"Then you have him spin some tale no one in their right mind would believe," he continued.

"He was returned in the same way he arrived."

"Do not interrupt!" The Governor set his glass on the table and leaned towards her. "Now, your enemy has come for you. We stopped being afraid of your kind long ago."

"Then you are foolish."

"We have a treaty and you will abide by it." He stood up and motioned for the servant to get his coat. "Deal with it and make sure no one in my city is caught up in your mess."

As he left the study, Queen Erena gripped the fabric covering her thighs and clenched her teeth. This was not how it should have turned out. Keeping human relations was her coven's, no her responsibility. She looked to her social advisor and the woman came to sit by her, patting her on the hand. "It'll be fine. He's human which means he's afraid of the unknown."

"We could wipe them all out so easily."

"But, where would all the fun be if we did that?

Exasperated, Queen Erena rose to her feet. She always saw humans as livestock until it became clear in this new millennia that they needed to co-exist. To this day she hated it.

"Come. We need to have a talk with Count Marchand."

The journey to the third Coven was an arduous one. It required going into the outer edge of the city. Within its borders sat Count Marchand's massive estate, overshadowing all the other expensive homes in the area. The rich liked the outskirts because it gave them unobstructed views. Not many wanted a landscape of the city regardless how beautiful it was at night when the lights flickered on. Having a coven deep in the knowledge of the new age made its location fitting.

Queen Erena leaned her head on the side of her window and looked up at the buildings as they passed them. She could never live in the city or its outer borders. Too much noise and the smell of blood from so many people would drive her insane. The fabric of her dress started to chafe and she wondered if she should have worn something more comfortable. Her social advisor had suggested the cotton acrylic blend attire, stating they should not 'stand out' even on the borders.

Her driver eased the Bentley up the third coven's driveway and swung in front of the steps leading to the doors. On either side of the entrance stood a sentry with an ear bud. The one on the left touched his, nodded, then came down the steps to greet her party.

"Good evening, Queen Erena," he cooed as she stepped out of the car.

"Count Marchand is waiting for us, I take it?"

"Of course. He had a feeling you may show up, though you could have called."

Queen Erena grimaced. She was fascinated with the telephone for about a quarter century. Then, it became a noose tethering her to everything and everyone. Her castle was out of tower range so when the new cell phones came out, she thanked her lucky stars. Although the land lines were still operational she didn't feel the need to call anyone herself. Her staff did that. Plus, some of the other covens were in the same thinking as her.

The last time she had set foot in the third coven, it was to meet with the new government leaders of the territory. She noticed some new things around the corridor plus updated furniture as they entered the sitting room. A waste of money in her opinion.

No one made quality furniture these days. Sitting down on the loveseat near the fireplace she undid the jacket that matched her dress and made herself comfortable.

Loud boots striking the marble floors echoed into the room and the doors on the opposite side flew open. A stream of servants carrying platters filled with drinks, finger food and snack cakes flooded the place and set them down all around. Plates were brought out and a perfect portion of each item was arranged on them before being brought to her people. The drinks were poured and the army of servants quickly dispersed, exiting the room the same way they came in.

As they cleared the entryway, Count Marchand emerged followed by his advisors.

"Queen Erena," his voice boomed. "It's been too long since your last visit."

"Well, I'm not much on the city."

Count Marchand sat in the high back overly cushioned chair across from her. A prepared plate she hadn't noticed sat on the end table next to him and he plucked one of the large grapes from it.

"Ah, but you should be. It's not so hard to get set up. With the advanced communications, these days even the most obscure locations can be connected."

"Yes," Queen Erena said slowly. She lifted her drink and took a sip. Hot totty.

"I can guess why you're here." He had a mischievous smile on his face.

Whenever he came to the coven meetings out in the castles, he was so well mannered and quiet. His persona changed with his environment so in his own abode, he was a bit jarring for her taste.

"Is that so?"

"The Governor was quite rude when he came to demand a meeting with you some days ago."

"It's about," she started.

"The enemy airships," he finished for her. "And, he is right to be worried."

"I have never known them to attack humans who were not involved in our cause."

"They have not attempted another attack due to that but, I think they are going to come up with a plan that would include a percentage of collateral damage."

She halted her cup midway to her lips and her eyes grew wide. This was not part of the deal. She had no desire to protect humans. Count Marchand let out a laugh and continued. "Oh, I understand your feelings completely. In their misguided authority, they have forgotten what we are, thinking us chaste and complacent."

"I do not want to engage in two wars on the same front."

"What on Earth did your daughter do to that poor young man? The Governor threw some muttered rant in about that too."

"Nothing pretty, but nothing we couldn't fix."

Count Marchand harrumphed and shoved a whole small cake in his mouth. As he chewed, his eyes locked in on her social advisor's lap. The woman was not looking up, concentrating on what to eat next from her plate. She suddenly tensed up and frowned, glancing over at him.

Oh, for the love of! She thought, not finishing it.

"Anyhow," Count Marchand said. "We must come up with a way to limit the casualties in our favor. Their percentage may be much higher than what we may find acceptable." His eyes never left her social advisors lap even as she glared at him. So much for his civilized demeanor. That is what irked her about Count Marchand. She couldn't predict what was going on in his head. Right now, she did and berated him in silence that there was no time for such vulgar activity.

"So we are not going to erect a shield structure around the city to protect the livestock?"

Count Marchand's green eyes brightened until they almost glowed. His smile took on something sinister and she sat back in slight fear. He grabbed his drink and chucked its contents down his throat.

"My dear Queen, you should know better than that. We're supposed to be vampires. Plus," he waved his hand, "putting up such a structure would take massive amounts of material and energy that I have no desire to expend on these humans. They are but a tiny blip in the human population." A small puff of air swept her hair back and she saw the Count leaning over her social servant like a cat about to lick a bow of cream. To her horror, his tongue did come out and run along the woman's cleavage.

"Count Marchand! Control yourself." She sneered, cup still in hand as she bared her fangs.

"Why should I? She's not mated to anyone, correct?"

"How about my consent first?" Her social advisor snapped.

He sat up looking a bit offended then laughed.

"Maybe later then." He went back to his chair and her advisor was able to sit upright again.

Queen Erena cleared her throat and set her cup, now empty, back on the table.

"Then, what do you propose?"

"Maybe in a day or two you could have her come by and stay the evening?"

"The human issue, you pig!" Queen Erena yelled.

The room went quiet and she felt the mood turn sour. She closed her eyes in shame and when she opened them, the Count was staring at her with glowing eyes, blood rimmed irises.

"My apologies, Count Marchand. I am just." Her hands balled up in her lap.

It was unbecoming of her as a Queen to show such hostility towards another coven leader and emulate weakness at the same time.

"Maybe you're the one who needs to be bed." His tone was vicious.

Her two enforcers reached into the jackets, grabbing the hilt of their guns. In a state of panic she stood and held up a hand to them. Count Marchand sat further back in his chair, amused.

"This has been entertaining, Queen Erena, but you should go home and rest. You seem run down from all this. Let me deal with the humans for now."

Her insides twisted tight like a rag being rung out. What he suggested meant she would no longer be the liaison which lowered the status of her coven. She was about to protest when she realized more of his cabinet had infiltrated the room and surrounded the entire perimeter.

"I really insist, Queen Erena. No offense. I don't mean to do you a disservice."

Enforcers came to escort her party out, her jacket held out for her. She snatched it out of the servant's hand and walked towards the door. A yelp from behind made her turn around to see her social advisor being held back by two of the Count's servants.

"What do you think you're doing?" She turned around to advance.

Swords unsheathed and positioned not far from her neck. She counted five in all and her enforcers had drawn their weapons as well.

"I require her insights and reports. Don't worry, I will return her as she was received. I'm not an animal, Mon Cherie."

"Don't do this."

"Go home, Queen."

He left the room, her advisor towed behind him by the two enforcers. When the doors slammed shut, the cabinet members smirked at her as the enforcers forced her and the rest of her party out to the driveway where her car awaited. Inside the car, she waited until it pulled off and cleared Marchand's property before screaming in frustration. She thrashed about, disregarding the other passengers as they tried to maneuver out of striking distance in the cramped space. Her eyes glowed with hate. Her reign had been usurped.

Ambrook Coven

Chancellor Rayne swiftly walked into Count Ambrook's study with a look of crazed indignation on his face so he waited for the man to get his bearings.

"What brings you here unannounced in such a state?"

His Chancellor stepped in front of his desk and laid both hands on the surface, leaning forward.

"Count Marchand has gone mad."

Count Ambrook reared back from the vocal assault.

"Explain."

"As the liaison to the humans, Queen Erena went to request assistance from Count Marchand in regards to the treaty."

"That sounds reasonable."

"He stripped it from her along with her social advisor, stating she no longer had need for such things."

A burning grew within him and he cursed himself for not seeing this coming. He knew all too well how devious the deceptively quiet Count was.

"Wait. How did he manage that?"

"By force. From what I understand, his entire cabinet and high level enforcers ambushed her in his sitting room holding swords at her throat until she complied."

Count Ambrook shot up from his seat. That was not happening on his watch. As the new leader of all the covens in the territory he was not going to tolerate them preying on each other for power status. With this new development, he had no choice but to lower Queen Erena's coven until the issue could be resolved. Once again, he would have to call a coven meeting to cauterize the fresh wounds such a maneuver would cause.

"Goddamn him!" He slammed a fist on his desk.

His Chancellor caught his glare and they stood looking into each other's eyes, an unspoken mutual rage conveyed between them. Breaking the connection, Count Ambrook walked around his desk and went through the still open door, his Chancellor close behind.

Coven School

Hearing the news of her coven's situation, Princess Adelia flew into a rage, her guardian barely able to keep her contained in the corner of the study hall while the rest of the group watched in pity. He understood her pain and cursed Count Marchand. The Marchand twins and the rest from that coven steered away from her immediately, fearing she would come at them and they were correct.

"We do not agree with our father's decision, you should know that," Olette said.

"It is counterproductive and crude," Olivier added. "This was not the time for such a move."

"On the other hand," he began, flinching at the Princess' primal scream as her blood eyes stared at him. "Our father is probably the only one who can come up with a remedy. Your mother should focus on keeping her coven safe."

Princess Adelia got out of Lariod's clutches and went for them. She got within a few feet of striking when one of the Marchand coven members backhanded her, sending her into a sideways flight across the room. She hit the bookshelf section along the path and slumped to the floor.

"Stop being a spoiled, petty brat!" The one who hit her was a woman nearly twice her size. "I am so sick of hearing about your rants, tantrums and disgusting escapades. You've grown very little in your way of thinking. A great fighter you may be, but your personality still stinks."

Lariod winced at the harsh words, knowing how right they were. His charge was still learning and he thought they should give her some slack but there was no time for that.

"You don't get to take advantage of her pain and treat her like a child." He went over to retrieve his Princess. "Like you, she was disinterested in the ways of our kind. You have no right to be high and mighty when you also need to grow up." Hauling her limp body to a chair, he turned to Chase. "Am I right?"

"That's right. No one gets to lord over anyone here." He came over to them and knelt down in front of Princess Adelia. "My father will fix this, but for now, we need to find a way to defend our lives and those of our covens. Infighting is not an option. You understand?"

His voice was low and reassuring. Something Lariod was never able to do for her. She lifted her head up and the bloody tears had dried in streaks down her face along with snot and drool. Very un-princess like in appearance. Another coven member handed him a wet cloth and when Chase moved out of the way, he began wiping her face clean.

They continued the meeting, going over strategies and getting their history professor to chime in on their progress. Princess Adelia sat silent through the entire thing. After it was adjourned and everyone had left the room, he picked her up. Carrying her down the hall to the stairs leading to the housing complex, he kept his feelings bottled up. Once he entered their room and laid her down on the bed, he immediately exited, closing the door softly.

There was an empty field on the other side of the South wing that he used to practice his sword techniques. Stepping onto the soft turf, he too let out a yell of pain and rage. He did that a few times before his body rebelled and slumped down to his knees. A feeling of responsibility came over him. As if he could have prevented the incident from happening by being there.

"Are you done?"

The voice was fairly close and familiar. He turned. Demitri stood behind him with arms folded across his chest and, was that look disgust? Disappointment? Angry, he stood up and faced him. To his surprise, the other vampire unsheathed the sword he had been carrying at his hip.

"Your clan doesn't fight with swords," he spat.

"I know." The vampire's voice was barely above audible.

He unsheathed his own sword and got into an offensive stance. His opponent readied himself for defense and he noticed how solid yet not quite right his stance was. A crowd had formed all of a sudden and he felt a sense of nervousness. Distracted, he didn't see the guardian lunge at him and almost lost his balance as he blocked the strike. As he regained his posture, the vampire was again mere inches from him.

How fast is he?

For the first time in a while, he struggled to get a vantage point on his assailant. Bad form or not, Demitri was definitely a fighter. He knew right then, that he couldn't lose his sword, the only advantage he had over the vampire. His unit had been trained in hand to hand combat but this fighter was from the slums, a street fighter with no rules of engagement except to win.

The duel went on for what felt like an eternity, draining his reserves until he somehow tripped backwards falling on his ass with the tip of a sword at his neck. He raised his hands in defeat and found himself breathing harder than he should be.

"Better?"

Demitri sheathed his sword and held out a hand. He took it and was pulled up. Everyone clapped, the sound harsh in his ears as the blood rushed through his head making it feel clogged with cotton.

"I guess so." He brushed the dirt from his backside. "Your form is horrible."

"I beat you."

"I was preoccupied."

The guardian turned away from him and walked off. "I know."

It finally struck him what had happened and he laughed. He did feel better after getting the kinks worked out of him. Losing his resolve was not an option. The enemy would take whatever opening they had if opportunity knocked.

Reenergized, he picked up his sword and sheathed it. A calm claimed him. Before the end of the week, if time per- mitted, he would find Demitri and give him some sparring lessons. If he was that well composed with bad stance, then it was safe to mention that he would be unstoppable with some pointers.

Ambrook Coven

With the debacle between Queen Erena and Count Marchand, Count Sapienti wondered what kind of united front they would have in lieu of it. He was quite angry about the whole thing as were the other covens but Count Marchand had no qualms about it. Inside his limousine were four of his cabinet members and two enforcers, the standard entourage. Queen Erena had gone into the mess as such. He frowned.

Count Ambrook's castle loomed above them and he sighed. Another coven meeting this time stemming from the recent incident. From his viewpoint, he saw Count Marchand's vehicle already pulled up ahead of them and emptying out. The smug look on Count Marchand's face made him want to get out and punch the vampire into the ground. Queen Erena's social advisor came out of the vehicle weary, pale and in obvious pain.

When their driver moved the vehicle up and away from the entrance so his could pull up, he opened the door and leapt out before anyone could protest. With one swift move, he caught hold of the social advisor and yanked her out of the Marchand's formation. Count Marchand whipped around to retrieve his new toy and was stopped cold.

Count Ambrook's enforcers were on him in seconds, swords unsheathed. He raised his hands and smiled. Turning back around, his party continued into the castle unfazed.

"What are you doing?" His head enforcer hissed. "That was dangerous, my lord."

The social advisor shivered in his grasp. From seeing her up close, he knew what Count Marchand had done to her. Probably an attempt to make her spill the Queen's secrets that had no pertinence on his task regarding the enemy.

"I was not going to let him have her one moment longer."

"My lord," the enforcer protested.

"If he had done the same to mine?" Count Sapienti asked angrily.

"Then we would be at war with Count Marchand," his military advisor said.

He kept a tight hold on the social advisor as his group made their way into the castle.

"I can make it," she whispered to him.

"I don't doubt that, but let's leave it at." She gave a little smile.

Count Ambrook watched from his study's window as the coven leaders and their entourage filed into the castle. Seeing Count Sapienti snatch Queen Erena's social advisor right out of Count Marchand's group, he had let out a loud guffaw. The look on Count Marchand was priceless, well worth the trouble it may cause, but he brought it on himself. Queen Erena's Bentley came around the bend, having missed the show and a new sense of agitation enveloped him.

She seemed to have aged a bit, the troubles surrounding her taking a toll. He looked up at the enemy airships still hovering above their territory and parts of the city. With a silent prayer to the children working diligently at the school, he went to greet his guests in the banquet hall.

First on the agenda was to clear the air about the altercation between Count Marchand and Queen Erena. He could tell from the looks on the coven leaders' that it was also on their minds. The banquet hall filled and he waited for everyone to be seated before speaking.

"It appears we have a new wrinkle in our plans with the human's government demanding some kind of protection. As much as I despise them, we cannot lose our territory." He noticed the nods of agreement and continued. "On another matter." His audience perked up, their expressions morphing into agitation. "We absolutely must not antagonize each other. I do not condone what you have done, Count Marchand, but since you now represent us I expect optimal results."

Count Ambrook saw that Queen Erena's social advisor was by her side and let out a sigh of relief. Nonetheless, a matter he would have to deal with after the meeting. His wife squeezed his hand and he took a deep breath. Letting it out slowly, he began his rant to lay down the law. They could not afford another incident like that.

Count Sapienti felt Queen Erena's presence float up next to him and he slowed down his pace. Her voice was low, filled with weariness.

"I thank you for returning my advisor to me."

"It was the least I could do. Opportunity was open."

"She is," the Queen started but didn't finish.

"I know. And you are not allowed to retaliate in kind."

"It boggles my mind how such a soft spoken, often demure, man could do such a thing."

Queen Erena let out a loud hiss that made him stop along with his group.

"He is not what he seems in the public eye. He only reveals himself to certain people and usually only within his realm."

Count Sapienti was stunned.

"Do you mean his demeanor is a facade?"

Thinking back to when he snatched the advisor from him, Count Marchand did turn around with an intent to do battle, his eyes burning with evil. A look so very out of place for the vampire he claimed to know.

"Very much so."

"That is a problem." He walked into Count Ambrook's sitting room as he said this.

"Indeed, it is." Count Ambrook said.

He turned his head towards them as he stood at the window staring at the enemy airships.

Only the coven leaders were allowed in this meeting, and all eight barely fit. If the lower house coven leaders were with them, a bigger room would have been necessary.

"So many gatherings in one day, Count Ambrook. What are we discussing now?"

"I have an update from our children through the school task master."

Count Marchand's eyebrows raised and Count Grieger snorted. He tried to put out of his mind what those two were thinking. As the two tech savvy covens, they were starting to make him feel distrust.

"The shields are not enough."

"Obviously." Count Grieger replied with a florid hand. "The other part is formation of the soldiers. We never really needed much of that since as vampires, we hunted independently and when the enemy attacked long ago, it was do or die."

"Yes, and because of that, I have been having my soldiers training in formations," Queen Erena said. "I believe four other covens are doing the same." She looked around for confirmation and got it.

Count Sapienti sat back and watched the meeting with a muted sound. He was no longer paying much attention, instead thinking of his coven. He did not have soldiers per se, but enforcers. In the bowels of his castle were some of the most ruthless fighters and he now had to face the truth how much he needed them. His tyranny was coming to an end.

It was never his intention to oppress the vampires in the slums but give them an incentive to climb up the status ladder. About a third of them were half breeds; half human or half werewolf.

"And your take, Count Sapienti?" Count Ambrook asked him.

He looked up from his reverie and saw that the conversation had moved into a different topic and he had no idea what was being discussed. Relenting, he shrugged.

"My apologies, what is the concern?"

"If you're going to be rude and not take this meeting seriously, then maybe you should exit." Count Grieger yelled at him.

"You do not dictate my guests in my castle!" Count Ambrook turned to Count Grieger. He then looked at him. "Evacuation of the city if necessary."

"No."

He said it so abruptly that some of his colleagues reared back in offense. The thought of organizing such a thing made him ill. Everyone in the room stared at him and he felt an explanation was in order. Off in the corner of the room he saw Count Marchand give a tiny smile. The man knew what he was going say and probably agreed. He continued his answer.

"How many in the city? A population of a little over three hundred thousand? If the enemy hits it, the casualty rate would be about thirty percent. If for some reason it seems like the enemy is going to wipe it out, the percentage flips," he pursed his lips and let out a small exhale through his nostrils. "We put them out of their misery. It would give us enough energy to battle for days on end with an added feeding supply for our two ancient ones."

He saw some of the leaders start to salivate at the sheer possibilities until Count Marchand cleared his throat to interrupt their daydreams.

"That is a viable option, to be certain, but we have a treaty with the humans and an entire city disappearing would alert higher authorities. I would like to keep out anonymity within this region."

And he was right, of course. Count Sapienti nodded slowly. It was the twenty first century and things had changed drastically. They had witnessed the de-evolution of man into wars and social injustice that made their eras seem tame.

"How long do we have?"

Count Ambrook tapped a pen on his desk.

"From what our children report, having a vantage point to observe the enemy at their location, a week. Possibly ten days. The airships have been moving into a new formation in small increments so as not to alert us. Their weapons bays are glowing in preparation for another assault."

"Can they do this? Make a plan in such short time?"

"With our help, I believe so. Who has not contributed to our efforts?"

Count Ambrook's expression turned deadly as he scanned the room. Count Marchand feigned ignorance while Queen Celeste and Count Brownlee wrung their hands together in various nervous motions. Count Grieger turned away when his gaze landed on him.

"I guess that means we are going on a field trip in the morning."

"What?" Queen Celeste sat upright in her seat.

"That is not an option!" Count Brownlee roared.

The meeting fell into dissention and Count Sapienti pressed his fingers to bridge of his nose. He eyed Count Ambrook from his upwards glance and saw him grimace. He reached for the gavel and slammed it down on the table. The arguments died as everyone jumped from the sound.

"It is not up for debate. No one leaves this castle until then and after we assist our offspring, you can go on your way. That is all."

Count Ambrook got up from his chair and quickly left the room in obvious disappointment at their behavior. A loud gasp got his attention and looking over he found Queen Erena with her talons in Count Marchand's throat. Not deep, but definitely far enough that he dared not move.

"Return her as she was received? Isn't that what you said to me?" Count Marchand's eyes grew dark as he looked into hers. "You ravage her like an animal and nearly drain her. How do you justify that, Count?" She seethed, drool forming at the corners of her mouth.

"How despicable. You can't accuse someone of his caliber to something so barbaric." Count Brownlee stood up ready to intervene, appalled.

"Not becoming of a Queen, that's for sure. Your advisor is probably lying." Queen Celeste added.

"She must have had a run in with one of your men, Count Marchand." Count Durante said. "But even so, that means you did not secure her safety within your own home."

The leaders who spoke against Queen Erena halted their berating. To let something like that happen to another coven leader's cabinet member in your abode smacked of disrespect and lack of kinsman ship. Count Marchand was visibly angry but he could see him struggling not to reveal his true nature. Seeing the situation may get out of hand, he went over to them.

"Come away, my Queen," he whispered in her ear.

She hesitated, her talons shifting slightly making Count Marchand wince. He laid a hand on her shoulder and her arm relaxed. Black talons retracted, leaving small holes in the Count's neck. The moment he was free, he backed up away from her, fuming.

Count Sapienti led her out of the room and noticed Count Durante and Count Grieger follow.

So, they also know about him.

He made his way back to the banquet hall where more food and liquor than a super market was being served. They were going to need sustenance for the long day ahead.

FOOLISH PLAN

The horizon lit up, a sea of orange and green from the air ships' acidic spray making contact with everything on the ground. In the poisonous mist, humans ran for cover. Some did not make it very far as they dropped from asphyxiation, their lungs turned to Swiss cheese by breathing in the mist. High above, the enemy air ships moved forward, inching closer to the other side of the city where the vampires waited.

Chase raised the binoculars to his eyes and focused on the air ships. They had spread out farther than he had calculated but still within range of their assault. He scanned the smoldering grounds of the city and rural areas. From where he stood on the top of his castle, he could see the shields holding up around the other covens in the distance. It was the least Count Marchand could do considering his personal vendettas.

Baltise sat in female form napping on the stone platform next to him. He had fed her well earlier. Queen Erena had still not revealed her Kataling but from the descriptions in the old text, he didn't want to see it anytime soon. Compared to that thing, he felt his Volshin was beautiful.

A ping in his ear made him place his hand over it on instinct. Count Seven could develop communication buds that worked in the countryside at long range so battles could be coordinated.

"You won't believe this," one of Coven Brownlee's offspring said in his ear.

"Tell me." He braced himself for what was coming.

"Move to the other side of the castle and look towards my home."

He tapped Baltise who stood up slowly and followed him as he took flight to the East wing. They landed on the edge and he looked through the binoculars again.

"Son of a," he cursed.

The elders were supposed to leave all planning to their offspring but some of them were not happy about it and voiced opposition. His father had shut them down on moving on their own, or so he thought. There in his view was Count Brownlee sending his fighters out ahead of schedule towards the advancing enemy air ships coming from the mountains. He had a smug look on his face and from the top of his castle, he turned to Chase and leered.

He lowered the binoculars knowing it would end badly. Since the only way to get his fighters on the ground was to deactivate a portion of the shields, it would leave the castle vulnerable in that sector. A rectangle formed along the fifth floor and fighters jumped down to meet the enemy troops marching towards them. Nearly two thirds of them had jumped out when it happened.

The air ship farthest in formation opened its weapons bay and the surrounding ships tilted away at forty-five degree angles. It wasn't an acid bomb that ejected out but something far worse sailing straight through the shield opening on the fifth floor and into the castle. Those in mid jump and waiting behind were incinerated instantly along with the structure. The weapon continued its destruction, burning away everything as fireballs bloomed within every window. The castle rumbled before the bottom half turned to ash causing it to tumble down in a heap.

Count Brownlee tried to jump off with his entourage but it was too late. They leapt right into a giant fireball as it spat out from below. The fire went on feeding off its prey, its wrath contained within the shield. Smoke spewed out from underneath the castle signaling the fire had gone deep.

"Close off the tunnels!" Chase yelled.

"Gah!"

He turned to see a group of enforcers nearby and one of them was holding his ear where his communicator would be. The others had their eyes squeezed shut, wincing.

"Sorry."

"On it," he heard a multitude of voices reply.

A silent prayer went up for the BrownleeCoven while they all watched it turn to dust. He turned away and looked out to the opposite side where Coven Durante lay. From the faces on the soldiers standing at the ready on the roof, he knew they had witnessed the coven's demise too.

"Stupid." He chastised them in death. "Hold positions. We need to get them closer."

"That weapon was nothing nice," Count Sapienti said in his ear.

"No. But at least we got to see it beforehand. Can we still do it, Count Marchand?"

"Recalibrating now, young Count." He found the elder's tone condescending.

"Princess Adelia?" He waited for a reply and received none. "Princess?"

"What do you want?" She snapped.

"Are you in position yet?"

"Why would you ask me something so asinine? I know the plan!"

"Just," he started to argue.

"We are in position," her guardian answered. "Don't worry so much."

Enemy airships lowered their descent into the city making a beeline for Coven Marchand. The vibrations coming from them shook buildings to their foundations causing collapse. Even at a distance, Count Marchand's twins could hear the human screams of desperation and despair. That made them smile a little before they got serious and went to the task of setting up a perimeter for an assault in the town square.

Out of the corner of her vision, Olette saw government troops coming down an alleyway on the other side. She tsked and watched the artillery being hauled behind them. State of the art tanks rolled in heading to each end of the small city, potentially ruining her plan. Touching the ear bud, she called to her brother.

"We have a situation."

"I know. I saw them. Stupid humans."

"Shall we assist?"

"Hells no. Let them evacuate their own kind. We will wait until the enemy wipes them out to initiate our coup."

She smiled and continued to set up while waiting.

"What are they doing?"

Queen Erena white knuckled the stone edge of her castle's tower roof. She saw the human army rush into the city.

"Evacuating their people."

Her head enforcer shrugged.

"I can see that!" She hissed. "I meant with those?"

She pointed to the missiles being brought in on flat beds. A thought came to her that Count Marchand probably didn't give the humans any confidence in her kind handling the situation as she had promised and were now about to be annihilated.

"How long do you think they will hold out?"

Her social advisor brushed hair from her face as the wind picked up.

Air perfumed with rotting corpses and scorched earth from the acid bombs permeated their nostrils. Queen Erena retched once and coughed. It had been a long time since she smelled the scents of a battle field.

"If the enemy unleashes another one of those fireballs, not long."

As if on cue, the airships broke formation in that same forty-five-degree angle and the far ship glowed orange, engulfing the sky. The bomb hit a few miles from the troops on the west side of the city but its impact was much wider.

Soldiers in mid screams, leaned back shielding themselves with their arms, melted into nothingness. The tank behind them disappeared. Every structure in its path was scoured clean.

Queen Erena hung her head. Foolish. What did the humans think they would accomplish against an enemy they knew nothing about. Yes, the airships appeared to be standard but that was the ruse. She bared her fangs and let out a cry of pain then turned to her second in command enforcer.

"Go through our tunnels and infiltrate the city to see how many humans we can rescue. Stage them in the tunnels until this is over."

"As you command, my Queen." Her enforcer bowed and led her unit out.

With the last sword treated with the new compound every soldier from the three military covens made their way to the battle field as assigned. Enemy fighters were spat out of the airships like machine gun bullets and they landed silently on the ground. The ones that were advancing on Brownlee Coven were already being engaged and winning. What remained of Brownlee Coven's fighters had begun to retreat with nowhere to go.

Not bearing to see them wiped out, Chase made a decision and called out to Count Durante's cousin.

"Lord Piero. Would you be willing to assist in creating an escape route for Brownlee Coven's survivors?"

"Gladly," was his reply.

Relieved, Chase looked up to the burnt sky.

Everywhere Falson looked a battle was raging between vampire and enemy. The city had been razed but most of the population was safe underground. he crossed his arms and waited for until the large bundles being hauled into the open were in position. The enemy had tried to get rid of them but shields surrounded each one.

Here comes your surprise. He smiled to himself.

Demitri stood at his side prepared to defend him if the enemy got close enough to penetrate the shields. They held up pretty good from afar but at close range would crack like thin glass, shattering into energy dust. He found that out along with everyone else as the enemy decimated the rest of Coven Five. Now, his kind fought desperately to keep the enemy at bay. A weakness exposed, they would no doubt try to capitalize on it.

"How much longer?" His guardian fingered the hilt of his new sword.

Falson couldn't figure out the desire to use such a weapon. When Princess Adelia's guardian proposed lessons to him, Demitri seemed indifferent about it. The look on his face as he caressed the thing told him otherwise.

"They should be in position momentarily. Anxious?"

"Blood thirsty."

Shocked, Falson stared at him for a moment.

"Their blood is not very appetizing from what I heard."

"I don't want to drink it, just spill it."

"Oh." He nodded. "Noted."

The bundles were in position and the tarps drawn off. Sitting on platforms were huge cannons that resembled jet engines, their multicolored lights spinning as the power was initiated. Weapons recreated from schematics in the archives. The moment Count Marchand found them, he went into a fervor. A low humming reverberated through the land and the airships changed formation, spreading out.

"You can't run from this, monsters," he said to them.

Tapping his ear piece, he gave the order.

"Fire at will."

The cannons moved with the airships, targeting the lead ships one by one. When they locked on, the cannons fired. Massive blasts of heat and stinging particles shot forth hitting them dead on. The ship closest to his castle broke apart in a splatter of debris. Some of the enemy were falling to the surface having escaped instant death to be met by waiting vampires.

The airships were being taken down by the newly devised weapons that not only destroyed the ships but neutralized the acid bombs contained within. Count Marchand had a suspicion of what might happen if the ships were taken down but he never divulged it to the humans who learned the hard way.

When by a miracle of shots one of the humans' missiles hit one, the ship exploded, spraying acid bombs and their content across a two-mile radius. A gruesome sight as they landed on the prematurely cheering soldiers who then screamed in agony before turning into what resembled raw sewage.

One ship was knocked off course and came careening towards Count Sapienti's castle, gaining speed. As a last-ditch effort, the ship tilted awkwardly and its weapons bay glowed. Falson grabbed his guardian and headed for the opposite side of the castle, attempting to outrun it. They barely made it, the shields breaking with the sound of thick glass, while they both hit the ground. The ship cracked in half and one piece went sailing above their heads to crash a few miles ahead of them.

Then the battle shifted.

Chase pushed an enemy away from him with one foot and blocked the blow of another coming up beside him. He glanced up and grimaced. The rest of the main ships had retreated but the ones remaining adjusted their timing so that when their ship went down, their soldiers could eject before the cannon fire hit. He never thought they would sacrifice their precious airships. But that wasn't the problem. It was the fountain of enemy troops crashing down on vampires already in the midst of battle, making them outnumbered three or even six to one.

Because of this, he had to join in the fight. So far, his kind was holding up but the situation seemed dire. Off in the distance he saw his father taking down four enemies at a time, a madness raging inside him. Having never seen his father like that, it frightened him. So much so that he lessened his strength against his opponent for a brief moment and paid for it. The blade swept across his face and he managed to dodge it enough to only be inflicted with a gash from cheek to neck. Enraged, he went at the enemy with double vigor and tore the head off, tossing it aside. Five more of the enemy were coming for him.

Baltise was not far from his side and kept looking over her shoulder to make sure he was doing okay. She still didn't like fighting but knew she had no choice. The enemy was out to destroy all vampires and she couldn't let that happen. As hungry as she felt even after being fed plenty earlier, she remembered the taste of the enemy blood and cringed. It would sustain her but she wouldn't like it afterwards. From above, she saw a large clump of bodies coming out of the air, feet first towards the battlefield. The closer they got her body screamed at her to move. They were aiming right for their sector. She pivoted sharply and dashed to Chase, now seeming so far away.

Enemy bodies flew in three directions revealing Princess Adelia in the center of the fray. Four more were trying to get at her but she was too agile, prone to take flight and come back with deadly blows. It was her signature move and she used it fully with great success.

On the other hand, she was getting tired even after drinking some of her prey dry between fights like these where it was seven on one. The battle had been going on for days now with neither side caving in. Relentless attacks from both and the enemy was somehow getting the upper hand.

Without a sound, more came rushing at her and she braced herself. Two of the four were down but now five more joined the remaining two. It occurred to her that was the magic number; seven. She spat blood onto the already blood drenched soil and mustered up more energy, feeling it wasn't enough by the time only three were left.

Before she could turn to take down the one behind her, a blade protruded from her chest, stopping her cold. Her head fell back and at the top of her castle she saw her mother's face crumble. Then a scream that carried to her in the wind assaulted her ears as another blade came through below the other but from the front.

"My daughter!"

Heearing her mother scream, she smiled.

She does love me after all.

Her body went into free fall when the blades were withdrawn and she contemplated if she had enough strength to hang on for a little longer. Blood came over her in a wave, the assailant before her ripped in half and her eyes widened with confusion. The ground did not come to welcome her. Instead, she felt hairy arms fold around her. They morphed into tanned muscled skin and the deep voice of a werewolf, her werewolf, spoke to her.

"I have you."

She grinned, coughing up blood.

"I'm a little low.on iron today"

He looked down at her without smiling. She could tell he was angry, but wasn't sure who or what it was aimed at.

Queen Erena gripped the ledge, watching Count Durante's werewolf take out the rest of the enemy surrounding her daughter then catching her. He carried her off the battle field, morphing back into wolf form and running towards the castle. She didn't take her eyes off of them when she spoke.

"Release my Kataling."

Her enforcer blanched but bowed low and went into the deep part of the castle to do as she was told.

I didn't make it! Baltise yelled in her head.

Her arm was outstretched reaching for him even when one of the enemy's claws punched through her master's chest as he came down from above. She knew if his hand came out, her master's heart would be in it. Gripping the hilt of her short blade she threw it and her aim was true, hitting the enemy in the neck. His arm went slack letting loose its hand's hold on her master.

She caught Chase as he staggered backwards. Her hand pressed into the wound tying to slow the bleeding. His breathing became ragged so she laid him down gently and ripped open the throat of a downed enemy. She brought the gaping neck over his lips and squeezed blood into his mouth. The wound began to close. She crouched down to give him some leverage. When the blood barely trickled she tossed the body to the side.

Something pricked her so she looked over her shoulder to see an enemy had run a blade into her back. Already full of rage, her eyes blood red, she took hold of the knife and yanked it out. With one hand she lifted the enemy up off the ground. Her bloody wings sprouted from her back and her fangs protruded as her mouth spread wide open.

Her fangs came down on the enemy's neck, severing the head in one bite. Not wasting her prey, no longer of sane mind, her mouth covered the spurting stump and she sucked the body dry. Grey and lifeless, the body was dropped like a piece of trash

Her wings flapped, raising her off the surface as a large horde of enemy came rushing towards her at every angle. She kept ascending until her body hovered high enough to see the entire battlefield.

"Prey," she sighed. "Hungry."

Swooping down at high speed, she plowed through the enemy lines devouring as she went.

On the other side of the battlefield near Queen Erena's castle, a massive creature lumbered out of the lower bowels, its eyes scanning the area. The beast had skin the color of charcoal, sleek and hairless with knobby legs. Webbing connected all four limbs to the body making it resemble a giant bat on all fours. Beady glowing orange eyes and glistening white fangs completed the creature's features. The soldiers who had unleashed it hurriedly sealed the doors after it.

Sniffing the air, it caught a scent and shot forth into the advancing enemy. Blood sprayed upwards in the air along with a loud crunching sound as it had its feast.

Count Durante nearly gagged at the sight of the Kataling and the Volshin massacring their enemy.

He felt no pity, just in awe of the ancient species raw power. But even though they were cutting down many the enemy numbers were too great. They were getting hurt as fast as they could heal. The enemy was winning. Most of the vampires still in combat were trying to hold their positions while looking for a way to retreat.

A crackling voice in his ear broke his thoughts.

"Found them."

He had no idea who it was that spoke through the communicator but knew what they were referring to.

"Do they look hungry?"

"Oh, I would say so."

"Then lead them out."

Dreading what was about to happen he leaned over the balcony, his duty now to bear witness.

High pitched shrieks filled the air causing every fighter, vampire and enemy, to halt their movements. Many looked around then up at the sky. Faces of sheer terror came over the vampires. In the sky above were four fully grown Volshin, twice the size of Count Ambrook's little pet guardian. They split into pairs flying towards opposite ends of the battlefield. On the ground were a total of six Katalings that also split, going in three different directions. Their speed defied their size.

In a communal attempt to save themselves, the vampires hit the dirt face down right before the enemy could react to the creatures as they sped through. The vampires got their backsides raked by the onslaught but they didn't dare move. Better to be wounded than torn apart.

From her view high above Queen Celeste watched the enemy numbers dwindle rapidly. She smiled to herself for figuring out the location of the two nests and sending Count Durante's men to scout it. That made her feel better, knowing the tide had now turned. In response to the new threat, enemy airships reappeared and vacuumed up what remained of their troops. When not one enemy still breathing was left on the countryside, the ships flew off into the horizon.

The battle was over.

EVERLASTING

Shades of red from bright to nearly black painted every square mile of the battlefield. Vampires slowly raised themselves up, assessing the damage of their surroundings. Scattered across the land, Kataling and Volshin finished off their meals, each momentous bite shedding the monstrous aesthetic towards a somewhat human form. Snaps and cracks traveled along the countryside as they ate.

Tears streamed down Baltise's face as she nibbled on a piece of bloody bone with a good chunk of meat still on it. Her wings already retracted, the hunger subsided, she sat in a pool of rotting blood next to her master. Being in her other form hurt psychologically due to the downward spiral into oblivion.

She sniffed hard, not caring about the snot running down her nose returning from whence it came. After dropping the bone, she wiped her mouth with the back of her hand and took a quick glance over at her master on the ground.

Surveying the land, she saw others like her reverting back to normal. For once she was glad not to be the only one but at the same time felt a foreboding of what the clans had in store for her kin. Long forgotten memories came back in snippets but she pushed them away. There was no need for that. The Katalings made her flinch in terror at their form and size.

"Are you alright?"

Chase's voice was barely a whisper.

She turned to him a nodded. His wound looked less savage on the outside but she knew internally it was too great a wound to heal so quickly.

"I'm glad." He drifted back into unconsciousness.

Looking out onto the battlefield she vowed to become a voice for the Kataling and Volshin. No longer would she stay silent and let the covens do as they pleased.

Count Ambrook stepped over enemy corpses on his way to his son. He would have kicked them out of the way but didn't want to dirty his boots with such filth. The anger was still boiling deep within him. Because of the enemy, he now had to deal with clean-up and a handful of Volshin. One was bad enough.

All those centuries of the covens pining for the ancients to level the playing field in a fight and the moment they show up everyone reared back in disgust. He admitted they were not a pretty sight but their power was undeniable.

"How do you want to handle this, my lord?" Chancellor Rayne came up behind him.

"I think we need to contain them in the lower levels for now. They are used to that kind of environment."

"Hmm. Count Marchand would probably like to breed them for research."

He whipped around and came face to face with his Chancellor.

"I will not allow such a thing," he said through gritted teeth.

"I agree, my lord. We cannot let Count Marchand have his way."

The men continued their trek through the aftermath in silence until finally coming upon his son. He looked worse than Count Ambrook initially thought. His guardian sat dutifully by him, covered in blood.

"Can he be moved?" he asked her.

"If you do it very gently," was her soft reply.

It always amazed him how docile she seemed knowing what kind of species she was. He knelt beside his son and placed a hand on his forehead. Fever. Cursing inwardly, he stood up and motioned for his medical team to begin transport. The first lift off the ground proved painful as his son gasped in agony, forcing the two vampires to set him back down and rethink positioning. On the second try, they were successful in getting him on the makeshift stretcher and carried him off to the crypt. His guardian followed in silence. As they passed each other, he blinked in fear.

Was that my imagination?

The glare his son's guardian gave him was full of bloodlust. A warning of sorts. But why?

Queen Celeste heard Count Ambrook's private request in her earbud and went to task. There was a part of the underground tunnels only she knew about and that is where the ancient ones would be led. She knew what he feared and felt the same. Count Marchand was a menace they needed to deter at all costs. Her archers stood ready from the rooftop of her castle. Their bows loaded with tranquilizer darts filled with enough dosage to take down four elephants. She hoped it would do the trick. If not, they would have a horde of angry monsters on their hands.

"On my mark." They raised their weapons into position. "Fire!"

Dark lines streaked the sky above and the ancient ones paying no mind were struck, some multiple times. They dropped like flies, their bodies not quite fully human.

"Hurry!"

Her extraction teams flew onto the battlefield and quickly swooped up the ancients. When Queen Erena's Kataling was in the arms of one of her soldiers, he was knocked out of his grip by one of Queen Erena's enforcers. She frowned and looked down at the amazon warrior who in turn smirked, taking off with her prize. So be it.

Pillars of smoke hovering above the city caught her attention. Lips pursed into a thin line, she turned away. This was part of Count Marchand's doing but she along with everyone else knew he would never take responsibility for it. She scraped a patch of dried blood from her coat's lapel. It had been a long time since she fought in a battle and she forgot how messy it was. If the covens didn't come up with a solution to their own internal strife, there could be another one which she did not relish.

The Congressman sat on the edge of the sofa, hands gripping his knees as he leaned forward.

"Is it over? Are those airships and your enemy coming back for round two?"

The man was visibly angry and Count Sapienti did not blame him. Two weeks had gone by and no sign of the enemy but all were on high alert. He was there to soothe the city government officials as proxy to the now reinstated Queen Erena. The city council had vehemently voiced their disgust for how Count Marchand handled the situation.

"From what we know from the past, they will not be back for possibly a century. The only reason they attacked was due to intelligence that we no longer had a way to defeat them."

"And our city? It is no easy task to have our own military force. One that keeps quiet about our little treaty."

"You think your city is the only one that accommodates our kind?"

"That's not what!" Congressman snapped his mouth shut and huffed. "This country's government won't like it."

"Ah. Well, no need to worry. We will help you rebuild and keep them at bay. I assure you."

He waited for the Congressman to sit back and relax before speaking again.

"By the way, what did you say happened?"

Chase looked around the school's library and thought about what could be included. After so much resistance to being in the place, he realized its worth. He learned more than he bargained for as did the other high class offspring. A new rule was going to be implemented and he couldn't wait to see the looks on the coven members' faces when his father announces it.

Footsteps came up from behind him and he turned his head slightly. Falson ran a finger across the study table as he walked further into the room.

"So, you think this whole school thing will be beneficial to all the covens?"

"I do."

"Educating the lower class will do what, exactly?"

"I think a more unified coven will strengthen our kind. Don't you?"

Falson snorted. He sat down in a nearby seat and crossed his legs. Leaning back, he stared at the ceiling.

"I guess that would be good. The problem is not necessarily us, though."

Chase raised an eyebrow.

"What does that mean?"

"I found out a while back how much of a tyrant my father actually is and make no mistake, the rest of the coven leaders are not far from it."

"Tyrant is a bit much,"

"Really? When did you find out about the underground caves and tunnels?"

He frowned at that. It did leave a sour feeling in his gut when he thought about his guardian battling their own coven's lower class to near death for the status he now holds.

"Not long after you, I suppose. We'll have to remedy that by teaching even the lower class what it means to be in our covens."

"You have such high hopes. For an artsy trouble maker." Chase laughed then sat down in the chair next to Falson. "This whole thing is a form of art, isn't it? I do like to keep things aesthetically pleasing." He rested his fingers on the side of his face. "On occasion."

Falson saw something stirring in Chase's expression.

"What are you thinking?"

Chase's eyes gleamed, a sinister grin forming.

"We should take back our home world."

"You can't be serious?" Falson yelled, staring at him. "How?"

"With a plan, of course, you ingrate!"

"I am no more one than you! I meant by what means."

Chase smiled at that.

"The same way our parents came."

"And what? Pack up and leave Earth? All of us?"

"No!" Chase sighed.

"Even if we found those ships, there's no telling if the damn things are operational."

"That's what Count Marchand is for."

"We can't trust him!"

"Nor should we. But, the enemy will follow if they think that is the case. We'll take an elite group." Chase stood up and leaned against the window. "And, I have a feeling Marchand will more than comply."

Falson went to stand next to him. They both looked out onto the vast territory claimed by their kind so long ago.

"The elders will think you've gone mad."

"Hmm. This is only the beginning."

END

ABOUT THE AUTHOR

Hi there!

I'm Maquel A. Jacob. I have had a passion for the written word since the age of seven, reading everything I could get my grubby little hands on which included encyclopedias and the thesaurus. At twelve, I had my first encounter with a Stephen King novel and was hooked. I then became inspired to write my own brand of fiction, combining multiple genres to keep things interesting.

I am a HUGE Anime fan, love a great bottle of wine and rock out to heavy metal music. Green and lush Oregon is where I currently reside, spinning imaginary worlds in my head and daydreaming.

For updates, FREE short stories, Newsletters

...and more

Visit: www.maquelajacob.com

Like Maquel A. Jacob on Facebook

Follow on Twitter @Rachel_Robinso

Also find me on Goodreads

ALSO BY MAQUEL A. JACOB

THE CORE TRILOGY

BOOK ONE: CORE OF CONFLICTION

BOOK TWO: SEEDS OF CONVICION

BOOK THREE: BONDS OF CONTRITION

A CURVE OF HUMANITY

BOOK ONE: ORIGINS

WELCOME DESPAIR

A COLLECTION OF SHORT STORIES

COMING SOON

A CAST OF SHADOWS

CURVE BOOK TWO

AND TWO MORE COLLECTIONS OF
SHORTS!